The Cowboy's Vow

To Nancy –

THE COWBOY'S VOW

A RODEO ROMEOS ROMANCE

LEAH VALE

Enjoy!

Leah Vale

TULE
PUBLISHING

ISBN: 978-1-953647-34-4

PROLOGUE

Late Spring

"YOU CAN WORK with us, Mr. Neisson, or you can work against us—something I do not recommend. But standing to the side and doing nothing is not an option."

Ignoring the other suit seated at the interrogation room table and the county sheriff leaning against the wall, Ian Neisson kept his gaze locked on the striking green eyes of the black-haired beauty seated across the table from him as she spoke. It was clear FBI Special Agent Jessica Martin was the one in charge today. Had she not researched him—or his family, for that matter—at all before calling him in here? The residents of the Wright Ranch weren't exactly the *standing to the side and doing nothing* type.

He leaned forward in the hard chair, all too aware of the thick metal loop protruding from the tabletop to which handcuffs could be attached, and resisted the urge to bury his unshackled hands in his barn jacket pockets. "I'm still not clear on what you want from me, Special Agent Martin."

She leaned forward too. A shimmer of gold at her throat caught his eye. The neckline of the simple white collared dress shirt she wore beneath her charcoal suit coat had parted just enough to reveal a tiny gold horseshoe charm hanging from a delicate gold chain. For luck?

"We need access to the ranching and rodeo community in the area. According to Sheriff Jenkins, you're the man to give it to us," she said.

The statement made Ian jerk his gaze back up to hers. There was gold there also, and the hard glint it gave her eyes made him think she created her own luck. "*Access?* What sort of access?" he asked.

"The kind that will help us catch the rustlers working the Idaho, Oregon, and Nevada—ION—territory," she said.

Ian looked to Sheriff Alan Jenkins, who was watching passively. "The FBI investigates stolen cattle?"

Alan shrugged. "When they're transported across state lines they do."

Ian returned his attention to the agents and asked with no small amount of incredulity, "You want me to help you catch rustlers?"

"We will be doing the catching, Mr. Neisson," the other agent, Peter Beck, a thirtysomething personification of a cliché FBI agent said with no amount of condescension.

Ian halfway expected the slender, dark-haired man to reach into the breast pocket of his black, well-tailored suit jacket, produce a pair of sunglasses, and don them in punctuation.

Instead he simply arched a brow and stared steadily at Ian with intense brown eyes.

Ian wasn't impressed. "Leaving me to do . . . what, exactly?"

"This is your community, Mr. Neisson," Special Agent Martin said.

"A small community where the presence of two federal agents will not go unnoticed," Ian countered.

"Exactly." Special Agent Martin sat back. "Which is why we need you to facilitate our undercover operation."

Ian glanced again at Alan.

Alan shrugged in a *she's not wrong* kind of way and said, "She's right." The sheriff straightened away from the wall and hooked his thumbs in his utility belt. "You know as well as I do that while Oregon might not be the Wild West anymore, at least not most days, the rodeo folks and ranchers here in the high desert are a tight-knit bunch. They respect you, Ian. And not just because of your grandpa."

Special Agent Beck flipped open the file folder on the table in front of him and read from the top document. "Thomas Wright."

Ian opened his mouth to answer in the affirmative but the sheriff beat him to it.

"That's right. *The* Thomas Wright. And short of going straight to him, if the FBI wants to get close enough to the main players in the region to learn who is involved, they'll need you, Ian."

"I'm not convinced enlisting the aid of a family member of one of our susp—"

Special Agent Martin held up a hand and stopped her partner short, but not before Ian straightened in his seat, instantly on high alert.

"Excuse me?" Ian said. They suspected his grandfather of some sort of illegal activity? Ian's heart started to pound.

From fear or anger, he wasn't sure.

There was no doubt Thomas Wright was a hard man. He was not above holding a grudge if he thought he'd been wronged. But he lived his life by the cowboy code of honesty, integrity, and courage and expected those around him to do the same. There was no way he could be involved. He liked winning fair and square too much.

The woman across from Ian folded her hands atop the interrogation room table, the picture of icy control. Except for her eyes. The gold-flecked green glowed with a fiery intelligence and strength of will. "We have no suspects at this time. But what we do have is millions of dollars' worth of cattle, rodeo rough stock, and bull sperm going missing and then being sold to . . . well, that is what we are here to discover. If some of the ranchers around here have amassed their fortunes through illegal activity, we intend to uncover those activities."

Ian clenched his jaw. The only rancher in or around Pineville who could be described as having a fortune was his grandfather.

"And as I said, you can either help, or—"

"And as you also said, you need my help, Special Agent Martin." Ian had dedicated himself to his family's—and by extension their community's—welfare ever since his grandfather's prized bucking bull had trampled his mom. The agents had no way of knowing about the promise his mother had extracted from him before she'd finally passed, nor did he intend to tell them. He wasn't about to let them poke around in the lives of those he cared for without him there to keep them safe.

CHAPTER ONE

Five Months Later

WHAT HAVE *I gotten myself into?*

FBI Special Agent Jessie Martin squeezed and released the steering wheel of the unmarked SUV she'd borrowed from the sheriff's department. Though they had spent the majority of the past five months at the bureau's Bend office, she and Peter had set up a temporary office at the sheriff's station under the guise of being auditors from the state checking the department's books. Not at all a stretch considering both of their backgrounds in forensic accounting and law.

But rather than auditing the sheriff's department, they were actually poring over the currency transaction reports the local banks were required to file for every transaction greater than ten thousand dollars made by the area's ranchers.

Trying to get a grip on her breathing and heart rate, she stared out of the truck's tinted front windshield toward the front entrance to the quaint little Pineville Diner. Ian Neisson, the heir apparent to the Wright Ranch, had suggested they meet at the popular eatery.

Though there was street parking available in front of the

diner, she'd parked the black SUV in the middle of the grocery store parking lot at the end of Main Street. At 9:45 a.m., there weren't too many people on the wooden boardwalk fronting the local businesses, their western facades on both sides of the two-lane Main Street. But there were more locals going about their business than she would like. She and Ian really needed to be cautious about being seen together, and she was beginning to think the choice of their meeting location was a mistake.

But not nearly as big a mistake as her seeking Ian's help in the first place. He was, after all, the quintessential cowboy. The exact type of man she'd left home to get away from. The type who put his dedication into his land, livestock, or rodeo career above all else.

What was that saying about best laid plans? She'd intended to live and work in the big city. Any big city. She didn't care which one, as long as it was the opposite of the remote isolation of her childhood. She'd graduated from the largest university and law school she could afford and jumped at the chance to work for the bureau when the opportunity presented itself. But as soon as her superiors learned she had grown up on a remote Nevada cattle ranch they'd wasted no time assigning her to the task force investigating interstate transportation of cattle, which led to her being sent here.

And she would be stuck in little Pineville, Oregon, with her fellow agent, Peter Beck, until they dug up enough evidence on the multimillion-dollar cattle rustling operation in Idaho, Oregon, and Nevada—collectively known as the

ION territory—to garner interest from the attorney general's office.

It was a task that was proving difficult without going undercover, which they couldn't do without SAC approval. And without an assistant attorney general on board, the special agent in charge wouldn't approve an undercover operation. Even after one of the men Ian had facilitated in the arrest of had claimed there was an electronic record of the livestock thefts held by "one of the rich guys."

She could be stranded here forever, chasing her tail, unless she risked taking matters into her own hands. As much as she dared. Doing so would be worth the risk if it allowed her to get back to the city that much faster.

Barring the modern-day rustlers driving their stolen herds down Main Street or hawking filched breeding straws on the boardwalk right in front of her, she had no choice but to work with the handsome cowboy, who, despite what she'd told him during their first meeting, would remain on her suspect list until she had concrete proof to the contrary.

She released her grip on the steering wheel, swallowed down the displeasure bubbling up inside of her, and exited the SUV. Though she'd dressed in hopefully less conspicuous jeans, a long-sleeve white Henley, and a tan leather jacket that matched her well-worn cowboy boots—the only thing she'd kept from her days on the ranch—she still kept an eye peeled for anyone who might notice her as she made her way to the diner. Fortunately the few people going about their business on Main Street didn't spare her a glance.

She entered the modest-sized restaurant and paused to

allow her eyes to adjust to the dimness after the brightness of the clear sky on this early fall morning. The décor was what she'd expect from a western-themed town's Main Street diner—wagon-wheel chandeliers, hammered brass accents, dark red faux-leather upholstery, and ladder-back chairs. A handful of empty tables filled the front of the space and booths lined the walls on either side.

Only two of the booths were occupied, both by people she didn't know. Not that she'd met many locals outside of law enforcement and a couple members of the Neisson clan in the five months she and Peter had been here. That wasn't their purpose.

The booths were being tended by a lone waitress. Jessie caught a glimpse of the line cook when he placed two food-laden dishes on the pass-through window counter.

Ian Neisson hadn't arrived yet. Not a surprise, seeing as she was fifteen minutes early.

Heeding the *seat yourself* sign on the hostess's pedestal just within the threshold, Jessie made her way to the very last booth on the left. The waitress, an attractive twentysome-thing brunette with an open smile, followed her to the booth. The name tag pinned on her white shirt read *Meg.*

Sliding onto the bench seat facing the door, Jessie de-clined the offered menus and ordered two cups of coffee. She didn't want Meg disturbing them while she convinced Ian to go along with her plan for gaining entry into the local ranching and rodeo world and hopefully discovering the whereabouts of this supposed record of the thefts.

Jessie had barely settled herself into the booth, pushing

the unnecessary utensils to the side, when Ian slid onto the seat across from her. He placed his cowboy hat on the bench next to him and ran a tan hand through his thick, wavy blond hair.

Just like when they'd first met, Jessie was struck by what a big man Ian Neisson was. While she'd seen his stats on paper—blond, blue eyes, six feet three inches tall, two hundred twenty pounds—nothing could have prepared her for the breadth of his shoulders, the sun-kissed streaks in his hair, or the crystalline depths of his eyes. The man had a presence to him that had nothing to do with his family's wealth or position in the community. Though, the circumstances surrounding his mother's death might have something to do with the deep lines bracketing his mouth.

Meg returned with two white porcelain mugs filled to the brim with hot black coffee. She lit up at the sight of Thomas Wright's eldest grandchild. "Hey, Ian! What are you doing in here so late in the morning?" Meg's gaze slid briefly to Jessie, the speculation clear.

"Hi, Meg. Just having coffee with a friend," he answered with an easy smile that didn't quite reach his eyes.

Meg didn't seem to notice, being more enamored with the motion of Ian's muscled chest beneath his chambray work shirt as he shrugged out of his oiled canvas barn jacket. Jessie had been that girl once. Never again.

The waitress nodded vaguely. "Ah." Another quick glance Jessie's way that had her wondering how a man like Ian—stunning good looks, wealthy family, and by all accounts, chock-full of integrity—remained single in such a small town. A mystery Jessie had no intention of solving. She'd already had her helping of cowboy back home on the ranch in Nevada. No, thank you.

Unfortunately, she'd have to stick close enough to Ian to prove whether or not Thomas Wright and the Neissons played by the rules. If not, it was her job to uncover exactly which rules they were breaking.

Meg lingered a moment longer in clear expectation of more information or maybe even an introduction, but when neither Jessie nor Ian said more in elaboration she said, "Alrighty. Just give a holler if you change your mind about eating or are ready for a top off." She gestured to their full coffee mugs then went to fetch the meals for the other diners from the pass-through.

"Mornin'," Ian said, his deep, rumbling voice drawing her attention away from the waitress.

Jessie met those compelling blue eyes of his. "Good morning, Mr. Neisson."

"Ian, please."

She acknowledged his request with a nod of her head. "Thank you, Ian, for agreeing to meet with me." She tilted her head toward the rest of the diner. "Charming establishment."

"I thought meeting here was wiser than me going in and out of the sheriff's station again. Me meeting a pretty lady for coffee will draw less interest than if I'm seen going to the sheriff's." This time, though the smile was slight, it crinkled the skin at the corners of his eyes.

Jessie brushed aside his pretty lady remark because he

was, after all, a cowboy who by definition was fluent in flattery. But she found herself snagged on the fact he was apparently in the habit of meeting with pretty ladies and that he didn't spend much time in the company of police. Because he didn't want to risk being associated with them? Or because he didn't want to risk slipping up and being caught in illegal activity?

"Where's your partner?" Ian asked.

She forced herself to focus. "Beck is at the station, reviewing financials."

All traces of his smile fled. "Whose?"

"I am not at liberty to say, Mr. Neisson."

He sat back against the padded bench seat and didn't remind her to address him as Ian. She couldn't say she was surprised.

"My family's?"

She couldn't deny it, so she simply stared at him.

"So why did you want to meet?" he asked.

"Because I still need your help."

His sun-bleached blond brows dipped. "You imply the FBI is investigating my family, even though we literally handed you Karl Fletcher after he tried to sell me stolen bull straws and attempted to hurt my sister, Caitlin, again. And after I called you for help retrieving my brother Liam's fiancée's stolen horse. Then, in the next breath, you ask for my help?"

"I implied no such—"

"Do me a favor, Special Agent Martin. Cut the crap."

Jessie reflexively glanced toward Meg, the cook, and the

handful of other diners as her heart rate spiked. None were paying her and Ian the least bit of attention.

She pulled in a deep, calming breath because Sheriff Jenkins's prediction had been correct. In the five months she had been in and out of Pineville, she had learned firsthand that if she wanted to get close to the main players in the ranching and rodeo community in the region, she would need Ian Neisson's help.

Folding her hands atop the table, Jessie said, "I'm sorry. Of course we are looking at the currency transaction reports for the Wright Ranch. I wouldn't be doing my job if we didn't."

He nodded, clearly already deducing as much. He didn't appear overly concerned. But it wouldn't be the first time she'd seen a cowboy lie with absolute conviction.

Devon had promised he would take her with him when he joined the rodeo circuit. Instead he took her beloved horse, sold to him without her knowledge by her stepfather. She had yet to forgive either of them.

"Exactly how am I supposed to be of help?"

"By giving me more, Ian."

"*What?*"

His incredulity gave her pause, but she got over it. She was going to bust the ringleaders in this rustling gang and earn an urban assignment regardless of what it might cost her.

"I NEED MORE, Ian."

Ian Neisson pressed his shoulder blades into the faux leather of the high-backed booth in the farthest, darkest corner of the Pineville Diner. Even with years of practice, he still had to do his damnedest to hide his churning anger from the stunning FBI special agent seated across from him. He slowly set down the steaming cup of coffee he'd yet to drink from. "I don't know what else I could possibly give you, Special Agent Martin. I've delivered Karl Fletcher—"

"Who used to work for your grandfather."

"Who stole from my grandfather and basically killed my mother to cover up the theft, then caused the death of my cousin and almost killed my sister to get revenge."

Ian could tell by the slight flattening of her lips that he'd failed to keep the anger from his voice. He decided he was okay with it. His family had been through hell because of the man this woman had just blithely implied was somehow in cahoots with his grandfather.

Out of the corner of his eye he noticed the line cook and the waitress look their way from where they stood talking through the diner's service window. At ten in the morning, with the breakfast rush of early risers over and the lunch crowd yet to arrive, the diner was mostly empty. Exactly why he had suggested meeting the FBI agent here at this time. Though discretion was paramount in his relationship with Special Agent Martin, Ian didn't care if his displeasure had been overheard.

Karl Fletcher, a former Wright Ranch hand, had cost his family so much in his attempt to deal in stolen rodeo rough stock and the frozen straws of prized bucking bull sperm stored within them. The agent's implication that his grandfather was in any way complicit made his blood boil.

Ignoring the waitress and cook, Ian continued, albeit a little quieter. "And thanks to the theft of Amanda's very expensive, and very noticeable, stallion, you were able to add the arrest of a high-end horse thief to your resume."

Special Agent Martin leaned forward and spoke softly. "I'm not here to build my résumé, Mr. Neisson."

While she sounded sincere, there was something in her green eyes, a shadow, that made him wonder.

"Do you know why I am in this oh-so-charming, rustic backwater town?" she asked.

Ian remained silent, pulling in a chest-expanding and hopefully calming breath, certain she would tell him.

"I'm here for the big kahuna, the head honcho"—she sat back and spread her hands wide—"the *man*. Whatever cliched, supervillain term you prefer. Because I assure you those reprobates who have done your family such harm were not the brains of the operation. They were simply grunts in a larger criminal enterprise. While their cooperation has been minimal, it is clear they were working for someone in the area. Someone who has thus far been very adept at hiding his involvement. And I intend to ferret him out and arrest him. Or her, if the case may be." She shrugged and folded her hands in her lap, very much a woman used to getting what she wanted.

"How do you plan to accomplish that?"

She leaned forward again. "Access, Ian. Access." Sliding

her untouched coffee cup to the side, she crossed her fore-arms on the table. "As I told you five months ago, I need you to provide me with access to the players in the rodeo and ranching community. Someone is making a lot of money off of the stolen livestock and straws around here. They are profiting from the blood, sweat, and tears of honest ranchers. I need to stop them. One way or another."

Ian twisted the plain white porcelain mug between his hands. "Why not simply subpoena all the records of the ranchers you suspect?"

She heaved a sigh and slid her arms back into her lap. "If only it were that simple. My job would be infinitely easier. More boring... mind-numbingly boring, but..." She shrugged and smiled briefly as if she meant it as a joke, but the hard, golden glint in her green eyes made Ian believe Jessie Martin had become an FBI agent for the more thrilling aspects of the job. He'd seen a similar look from the bull riders who climbed aboard the rank bucking bulls and broncs his family bred. The sort who lived for the rush of sticking until the buzzer sounded, more than willing to risk life and limb.

The things Ian was willing to risk to protect his family...

And at the moment protecting them, and the Wright Ranch, meant continuing to help Special Agent Martin. He couldn't allow any more attacks against his family, and catching those responsible would definitively clear his grandfather's name.

Ian circled back to her initial request. "What, exactly, do

you mean when you say you want me to provide you with access to the *players*"—he fought the urge to make air quotes around the word—"in the local rodeo and ranching community?"

"I would like you to help me be present when they go about their business. Show me places where these illegal purchases and sales might possibly be made. Get me close enough to see who might be paying too close attention to entirely legal sales that might tip off the rustlers to potential new scores, such as high value animals or even entire herds that could be snatched and shipped to states without brand inspectors."

"High value animals such as Amanda's Whiskey Throttle."

"Exactly like Whiskey Throttle, who was purchased at an auction. But luckily for your brother's fiancée, her new stud was chipped, and you alerted us before the horse could be transported out of the area. Most owners aren't as lucky." There was definitely a shadow dulling the glint in her eyes now. He'd never imagined feds to be so empathetic.

"And you'd like to stop the thefts before they occur."

The shadow cleared and she smiled again, a genuine smile that warmed her eyes, lit up her beautiful heart-shaped face, and hit Ian right in the gut. "That would be ideal."

Forcing himself to focus on what she was asking instead of how she looked asking it, Ian ran a hand through his hair. "I guess I could take you to the High Desert Livestock Auction. Introduce you around."

She glanced toward the pass-through window, but the

cook was nowhere to be seen and the waitress had moved away to wipe down a table across the restaurant from them. Clearly deciding they couldn't be overheard, she met his gaze again and said quietly, "But not as FBI, obviously."

"Obviously."

"You can introduce me as a friend from college who's in town to audit the sheriff's department—the cover we're using to work there—and curious about your ranch life."

"And your partner?"

"Special Agent Beck? He'll provide support."

"Because you feds think the old guys won't be suspicious of a pretty lady and will have looser lips?"

"Because I'm certified undercover. Special Agent Beck is not."

"Certified undercover?"

"I've completed the necessary training and earned the required certifications to operate as an undercover agent."

Ian nodded. He'd been right. Special Agent Martin was in it for the thrill.

He took a moment to roll what she was suggesting around in his head, adjusting his cowboy hat on the bench seat next to him. "What kind of friend?"

She settled back with a confident smile. "A good friend."

Ian ground his back teeth together. This arrangement kept getting worse and worse.

CHAPTER TWO

HER INSIDES A riot of anticipation, Jessie fidgeted in the passenger seat of Ian Neisson's huge black pickup truck parked in the mostly empty lot of the High Desert Livestock Auction. She checked her watch. They'd arrived thirty minutes before the scheduled start of the auction at noon to capitalize on the socializing that usually occurred before the attendees got down to the business of buying and selling ranch and rodeo stock. Fifteen minutes had passed, and while her impatience was already halfway around the proverbial track at a full gallop, the ranchers she intended to eavesdrop on were only now beginning to trickle in.

She checked the connection on the tiny digital video feed and microphone masquerading as a button on her brown leather jacket.

"That's the third time you've checked it, Jessie. Leave it alone. It's working fine. You're fine," Peter said through the tiny receiver tucked into her ear canal, well-covered by her hair. Though he'd parked the unmarked surveillance van a good fifty yards away, he sounded as if he were seated next to her. After following her and Ian from where they'd met up outside of town, Peter had taken a position near the road that would provide a clear view of those coming and going from the auction while remaining inside the van.

She pressed her lips together to keep from telling her fellow agent, on digital recording, what he could do with his reassurances. Especially when she knew she needed the reassurance. Not because she feared what she might encounter inside the auction house, but because she was going out on a limb by going undercover without SAC approval. This was the first investigation she'd worked with Peter, and the fact that he could already read her after only a few months added to the rampaging nerves wreaking havoc on her stomach. She diligently worked at being hard to read. Not only did it make her better at her job, but it also made her harder to hurt.

Sweat prickled the skin beneath her bra and her palms were growing damp. With a silent curse she wiped her hands on her blue jeans as surreptitiously as she could and glanced at Ian in the driver's seat. He looked as cool as a cucumber as he gazed out at the swath of blacktop.

Yet again she found herself thinking *What have I gotten myself into?* Just because she had all the training and had passed all the tests to work undercover didn't mean she had the practical experience. Plus, she'd never had so much at stake before—her career being one of her concerns. Her hand drifted toward the hidden camera again.

As if feeling her gaze, Ian shifted his attention from the parking lot to her. "Is that some sort of tiny camera?" Ian gestured toward the pseudo button, having obviously noticed her repeated fiddling with the tiny wires leading to the equally tiny battery pack tucked into her jacket's interior breast pocket.

"Audio/video feed. In the van, Special Agent Beck will see and record everything this fake button sees and hears." She used the truck's passenger-side mirror to check, again, the location of the van Peter was watching from.

"Is he recording now?" Ian asked.

"Why, is he going to confess?" Peter's voice, dripping with sarcasm, sounded in her ear.

Jessie ignored Peter and kept her expression and tone passive. "He'll begin recording as soon as we enter the auction house," she lied. The recording had started the moment she'd climbed into Ian's truck. Because Ian might actually confess in some way to involvement in the livestock thefts. One of her undercover operations instructors had once said a lot of people have a near-pathological need to confide in someone when they've done something they know is wrong. It was her job to be that someone. She mentally shrugged off the unlikelihood that Ian would be the type who needed to unburden himself. Those broad shoulders of his looked like they could carry a lot of weight for a very long time.

"Barn."

She had to shake herself from her wishful thinking and focus back on Ian. "What?"

"It's called an auction barn," Ian corrected her, his tone patient, and returned to watching the parking lot for the arrival of the livestock auction attendees.

Jessie looked out the truck's front windshield at the long,

low, dirt-brown building that more closely resembled a rural Elks Lodge than a barn. Only the slightly larger metal roofline attached to the back and the honeycombs of paddocks and chutes behind the buildings, along with the soul-penetrating smell of manure, revealed its actual purpose. But what did she know?

This was her first visit to an auction *barn*. Her stepfather had never taken her with him when he'd gone to auction back home in Nevada. She was realizing her lack of experience, both in actual, real-world undercover work and attending livestock auctions, could hinder her today.

She adjusted the camera button yet again as what could only be insecurity rose in her throat like heartburn. She hated the feeling. Insecurity meant vulnerability, and she'd vowed never to be vulnerable to anything, or anyone, ever again.

A long-suffering sigh sounded through the earpiece. "Stop fiddling, Jessie," Peter pleaded. "It's working fine. But it might stop if you keep messing with it."

She dropped her hands to her lap. Peter was right. The camera was fine. She was fine. She knew exactly what she needed to do and how to do it. Get close enough to the main players in the area's ranching and rodeo community to discover who was buying—or not buying—what from whom. The only thing she should really be worried about was accidentally letting her disdain for all things cowboy show. The urge to look over again at the poster boy for *The Cowboy Way* seated next to her in the truck took everything in her to resist.

Loosely twining her fingers together in her best facsimile of calm composure, Jessie returned her focus to marking the arrival of the area's ranchers in their trucks, many pulling empty trailers in clear anticipation of successful bids. But it didn't take long for her gaze to catch on the chiseled profile of the ridiculously handsome rancher seated next to her despite her best efforts.

His spotless cream cowboy hat was pulled low over his brow, as if to hide his identity—a pointless attempt considering *The Wright Ranch* was emblazoned in gold-tone paint on both sides of his big black truck. In deference to the crisp fall day he was wearing the same oiled canvas barn jacket he'd worn the day they'd met in the sheriff's interrogation room. Crisply ironed, dark-washed jeans encased his long, muscular legs. His brown cowboy boots were as well-worn as hers. Clearly he wasn't the type of rancher who spent his days behind a desk. That was his grandfather's job.

Jessie had yet to personally meet Thomas Wright, but she'd seen him from afar. The man was the successful rancher personified. Impeccably dressed with a high-end western flare, Thomas had a presence that came only with supreme confidence and excellent genes. Both of which had obviously been inherited by his eldest grandson.

Ian turned toward her, his blue gaze colliding with hers. For a heart-stopping moment Jessie was seized by the notion Ian could read her as well as Peter was learning to, that he knew what she was thinking.

"Are you ready to go in?"

She blinked, working to clear her mind of her irrational

fears. Glancing out the truck windows to the now nearly full lot, she asked, "Have the main players arrived?"

He blinked right back at her, but more slowly, as if clinging to his patience. "Well, I'm not entirely sure who, exactly, qualifies as a main player, but there looks to be a fair number of the larger local ranchers here."

"Enough that my presence won't be noted?"

A corner of Ian's mouth ticked upward. "Ma'am, I'm afraid your presence would be noted in a packed stadium."

Jessie opened her mouth then immediately closed it, unable to think of a response.

In her ear, Peter chuckled and said, "He's right, you know."

But she didn't want to be noticed. She wanted to observe and document, so she fished an elastic hair band from her jacket pocket and gathered her long black hair into a low ponytail at the nape of her neck. She met Ian's gaze expectantly.

His gaze traveled over her handiwork and her face in a way that made her want to fidget again. Then he shook his head in bemusement. "Sorry, didn't work." His hand went to the handle of the driver's-side door. "You ready?"

As surreptitiously as she could, Jessie pulled in a breath to calm the sparklers of sensation his inspection had set off under her skin and released it slowly. "Yes. I'm ready."

Ian gave her a quick nod and opened his door.

"Go get 'em, tiger," Peter said.

Watching Ian exit the truck and shut the driver's door, she softly asked Peter, "Were you noting the license plates of the vehicles as they pulled into the lot?"

"I was. As well as photographing the occupants as they enter the auction *barn*. As we discussed."

"Good. Just checki—" She cut herself off when the truck's passenger door opened and she turned to see Ian holding it wide for her. Of course. He'd rounded the truck and opened her door. In the cowboy way.

"Thank you," she said as she hopped from the tall truck, carefully avoiding his gaze. She still needed him to think of her as a sympathetic ear he could confide in. Not an FBI special agent with zero patience for cowboys.

Ian swung the truck door closed and stepped next to her, his elbow jutted out toward her.

He was offering her his arm? Of course he was.

Jessie bit down hard on the groan she desperately wanted to let fly and instead gave him a tight smile as she slipped her hand into the crook of his arm. Unbelievably, she could feel the heat and strength of him through his jacket.

Of course she could.

As Ian led her toward the unadorned entrance of the auction barn, joining the other ranchers and ranch managers still arriving, Jessie pulled in several additional deep breaths in an effort to achieve her *don't notice me* face.

Ian murmured, "You'll be fine. You have nothing to worry about. We're good people around here."

Sheer terror that he was reading her so easily turned her blood to ice. She glanced sharply at him, but he was nodding a hello at the two men who'd reached the door ahead of them and had paused to hold the door open, their curiosity blatant. Did women not frequent the auction barn? Jessie found the notion hard to believe considering the fact that women ranchers were not at all uncommon and women competed right alongside men in several rodeo events.

But as soon as they'd entered the long, rather narrow room that served as the gathering space and very informal dining area for the auction's café, and Jessie's eyes adjusted to the dimmer interior, she could see at least four women present along with the dozen or so men.

And man or woman, all eyes were glued on her and Ian.

Maybe the problem wasn't a lack of women, but rather a lack of women on the arm of Ian Neisson.

So much for her *don't notice me* persona.

She could tell by the sudden stiffness in Ian that he was also aware of the attention they were garnering.

To make sure she wasn't missing something, she murmured, "Why is everyone looking at us like we've just walked down the aisle?"

"Because I haven't had a . . . lady friend, if you will, for a while."

"How long is a while?"

"Ten years, give or take."

She quickly turned to look at him fully. "What?"

In her ear Peter said, "He's saying he hasn't dated since his mother was trampled by a bull at the Wright Ranch. She passed from her injuries about a year ago."

Jessie knew exactly which part of the file Peter was reading from, and empathy flooded her like quicksilver. Rebecca Neisson had clung to life, bedridden in various degrees of consciousness, for nearly a decade. Thanks to her father Thomas Wright's wealth she'd been able to receive the best professional care available at home in a specially outfitted room. But all that wealth had simply delayed the inevitable. Jessie's heart grew heavy with sympathy.

Ian glanced at her, then shrugged. "My focus has been entirely on the ranch and my family."

A family privy to every medical up and down his mother encountered, trying to cope with the reality of the sort of injuries a rampaging bucking bull could inflict. Coming to terms with the knowledge nothing would ever be the same, but clinging to what they had at the expense of any future hopes and dreams they might have harbored.

Far worse than the empathy engulfing her, a kinship with the gorgeous cowboy bloomed and clogged her throat. Not for his dedication to family—she'd run far and fast from her own—but the singularity of focus at the expense of his own needs.

She quickly squashed the sentiments stirred by the notion that Ian didn't have regular female companionship. It didn't matter and she didn't care. She. Didn't. Care.

The murmur of speculation from those eyeing her let her know she was alone in the sentiment. But she could use these people's assumptions to get closer to the community—and ultimately the main players in the region.

And all without feeling anything close to empathy or, god forbid, kinship, with Ian Neisson.

So she had no choice but to switch to *flirty charm*. She might as well run with the assumptions shining bright in the expressions of the auction attendees watching her and Ian. Smiling warmly, she twined her arm fully around Ian's and snugged herself up against him as close as she could.

In her periphery she saw him glance sharply at her, so she locked her smile in place and looked up at him to send him a quick wink. Hopefully he would wait until later to question her.

Though he returned her smile, his eyes were hard. Then his gaze shifted to where her ponytail had caught in the collar of her leather jacket, and he lifted a hand to smooth it back over her shoulder. Her heart did the thing in her chest she absolutely hated, pumping hard against her breastbone. Before she could attempt to read Ian, he shifted his attention to a table near the door piled with auction schedules and livestock descriptions.

While she was inclined to take him at his word regarding his social life because she had previously uncovered no evidence of Ian being involved in any sort of serious romantic relationship, maybe there was someone special in the community who he wouldn't want the gossip of her hanging on him getting back to. As the first ranchers broke away from the others and approached them she knew she'd have to wait until later to question him.

Ian extended his hand and greeted two older ranch-weathered men wearing jeans and nearly matching denim jackets, introducing her as his "friend."

Their grins and knowing looks deepened.

The shorter of the two, Chuck Anderson, who she knew to be a rodeo rough stock rancher, similar to Ian's family but on a much smaller scale, gestured to Jessie. "Why don't any of my friends look like that?"

The other rancher, Phil Trask, who raised angus cattle, barked out a laugh. "Because you don't look anything like him." He aimed a thumb at Ian.

And so it went as they worked their way around the room, weaving around the long tables and banquet-style chairs. Jessie appreciated how Ian made a point of introducing everyone to her by name to help her connect names and faces in real time. And making clear he really did know everyone in the area, as the sheriff had proclaimed.

Unfortunately, not everyone of interest to her was present. Wanting a moment with Ian out of the earshot of the other ranchers, she said, "How about a coffee to take into the auction with us?"

Ian glanced up from the schedule he'd picked up by the door. "Yes, ma'am."

Jessie's teeth were instantly set on edge. She could only handle being *ma'amed* so much. But for the sake of their audience she smiled sweetly at him and let him escort her to the café's order counter and pay for their coffees.

As soon as they were as alone as they were going to get while their coffees were being made, she asked him, "So Grant Williams isn't here?"

"No," Ian answered without looking toward the crowd who'd begun to queue in front of the door leading to what must be the auction arena.

"Is that normal?"

Again with the shrug. "He's a busy man."

Peter said, "Busy buying stolen rodeo rough stock from modern-day rustlers?"

She sighed, not just at Peter's nonessential speculation in her ear but at Ian's less than helpful response. A sinking feeling settled in her gut. At this rate she'd be stuck in cowboy land forever.

ANNOYANCE, HOT AND prickling, flared behind Ian's sternum. Not just at Special Agent Martin's unwarranted interest in Grant Williams, one of Ian's grandfather's oldest friends, but at his neighbors for assuming that the undercover FBI agent was anything other than an acquaintance with an interest in livestock auctions. He could feel their curious and practically giddy gazes on his back as he and the agent waited at the café counter for Mrs. Dayson to prepare their coffees.

He'd known her plan to go unnoticed would be an epic fail. He'd watched her as she watched the ranchers line up at the door to the auction arena. She was far too beautiful a woman to ever simply fade into a crowd, ponytail or no. She could have had a career in theater or film, and not simply because of her looks. As soon as it became clear they had the attention of the room, her posture, her smile, and even the glint in her eyes changed.

In a wink she'd transformed herself from the girl next door looking to experience her first livestock auction into a flirty vixen capable of teasing out any man's closest held secrets. He'd be wise to remember the sort of skills she possessed. Because she wasn't an actress. She was an FBI agent bent on digging up dirt that he believed in his gut wasn't there.

He knew firsthand that bad actors were in the area, but the FBI were sorely mistaken in their theory his grandfather or neighbors were involved.

Mrs. Dayson snapped the plastic lids on the disposable cups and slid them across the counter. "Here you go, dears." Then she looked pointedly at him. "Ian, I don't believe I know your lady friend here."

He opened his mouth to say his *lady friend* was simply a *friend* come to Pineville for work but Special Agent Martin stuck out her hand, her smile bright and engaging.

"I'm Jessie, ma'am. Ian and I were . . . acquainted, in college." She tossed him a very saucy wink. "He's agreed to let me tag along with him to see what, exactly, a ranch manager does so I'm not just stuck in my hotel."

Mrs. Dayton beamed at Ian as she shook the agent's hand. "That would be our Ian. It's a pleasure to meet you, Jessie. I'm Barbara."

"It's so nice to meet you, Barbara," Special Agent Martin gushed.

"Good luck in there today." Mrs. Dayton nodded toward the door to the arena just as it opened to admit the attendees. The waiting and dining space was instantly flooded with the earthy scent of sawdust and livestock. "But I sincerely hope we'll be seeing more of you around here." This time the look she sent him was downright hopeful.

Damn it.

Again, the agent beat him to the answer, which from him was going to be *Sorry, she's just here for the day.*

Special Agent Martin said instead, "I'm not going anywhere for a while, Barbara." She slid her gaze to his and her look was all law enforcement, compelling him to concur.

The words she wanted to hear were as thick as high desert dust in his throat, so he simply nodded.

As hot as his annoyance over his neighbors' assumption was, the guilt he felt for not being truthful to them made his chest burn like wildfire. But if going along with Jessie Martin's plan resulted in a speedy resolution to the investigation, he'd do it.

CHAPTER THREE

I'*M NOT GOING anywhere for a while.*

Jessie's own words echoed through her brain as she followed Ian into the auction arena, her coffee in one hand and the auction schedule in the other. She held her breath as much as she could to minimize the impact of the aroma making its way into the space from the holding paddocks undoubtedly right behind the arena.

It had been ten years since she'd left the ranch she'd grown up on, but the near-oppressive stench of manure still had the power to dredge up the disappointment and resentment that had driven her away. Away from all the cowboys who'd promised the world but delivered only dirt and heartache. But she loved her job, and her bosses wanted her here, in cowboy central, so she'd just have to make the best of it, manure and all.

Ian's broad back consumed her view and prevented her from getting a lay of the land as they stepped through the door between the dining area and the arena. But he almost immediately turned to the left to climb the stairs to reach the seating in what she discovered to be an indoor arena with the livestock corral at the bottom and ascending rows of bench seating rising upward. Despite the smell, the loose soil and sawdust mixture in the corral was clean, as was the corral's white metal tube railing and the solid gate through which the sale animals would be brought in.

While not an overly large space, at least a hundred people could be accommodated on the benches that wrapped around all but the whitewashed and advertiser logo-filled back wall where the auctioneer's booth was located above the small corral.

Today, less than half that number of people were present to see the livestock scheduled for auction. Not completely unexpected with rodeo season in full swing. All Jessie cared about was the presence of the wealthier ranchers in the area with the wherewithal to transport the sort of large numbers of cattle and horses being stolen in the region.

She followed Ian several steps into the highest row of seating with nothing at their backs but the wall, grateful he clearly recognized her need for a clear view of all the attendees while garnering the least amount of attention toward themselves.

He kept going until he'd reached midway down the unoccupied bench before he stopped and sat down. When she settled herself next to him, she realized she'd managed only one of her needs. Just like in the dining area, everyone was looking at them, heads bending occasionally toward their neighbors in obvious discussion.

She heaved a sigh and plastered a *golly gee, this is my very first livestock auction* smile on her face. While this *was* her first livestock auction, any excitement she might feel stemmed from the prospect of spotting one of her potential suspects.

To that end she purposely scanned the crowd, taking care to note the people she hadn't had the opportunity to meet when Ian had introduced her around the dining area. She slowly turned in her seat so the tiny camera on her jacket could pan the arena below her.

"He's not here," Ian said flatly.

She glanced at him and found him leaning forward with his elbows on his knees, his cowboy hat tilted low, studying the auction schedule in his hands.

She dropped her gaze to her own schedule as well, opening the tri-fold pamphlet and finding brief descriptions of the animals to be auctioned. "Are you sure?"

"Yep." But he didn't look up from the pamphlet.

"No vehicles registered to Grant Williams or his ranch pulled into the lot," Peter concurred in her ear.

Pretending to adjust her small hoop earring, she gave a single tap on the earpiece to send a soft ping of acknowledgment to Peter.

To Ian she said, "Is that usual?" She reframed the question she'd asked him while getting their coffees.

He slid her a look that made it clear he was quite aware she was asking him a question he'd already answered. "It's rodeo season."

Another way of saying Grant Williams was a busy man.

"Yet you're here," she pressed.

"Escorting you." His tone was pointed. He straightened on the bench and pulled in a deep breath as if calming himself.

Ian Neisson struck her as the type who didn't like to let what he was actually feeling show. The fact she could make him loosen his tight grip on himself could definitely work in her favor if the need should arise.

He refolded the schedule and set it on his muscular, jean-clad thigh. "Besides, as ranch manager at the Wright Ranch, it's part of my job to be here."

From what she'd learned about Ian Neisson since she'd met him five months ago, there wasn't much that he didn't consider part of his job. He ran the multimillion-dollar ranch for his grandfather, took care of his siblings, and kept tabs on the welfare of those in his community. Talk about an overachiever.

She'd just opened her mouth to ask him if Grant Williams's ranch manager was in attendance when a large male body plopped onto the bench next to her.

"Who's your friend, Neisson?"

Jessie turned and met the dark gray gaze of a very handsome cowboy with hair nearly as dark her own curling from underneath a tan cowboy hat. He looked to be roughly Ian's age, thirty or so.

A slightly younger version of the black-haired cowboy, no less handsome, slid onto the bench with enough enthusiasm to squish them all together. She found herself pressed tight against Ian and his heat and spicy scent completely emptied her brain for a solid beat.

"Yeah, Neisson. Who's your friend?" the younger one echoed with a grin.

In her ear Peter said, "Turn more and tilt back so I can see them, Jessie."

Which equaled her sticking her chest out at the two cowboys. Not freakin' likely.

Ian sighed as if a fly had just landed in his coffee, but she could feel his muscles bunch in tension where she was pressed against him.

"Garrett and Ben, meet Jessie Martin. Jessie, meet Garrett and Ben Hadley. Clearly, they are brothers, and part of the Hadley Cattle Company."

Jessie took the big, work-roughened hand offered by Garrett, the oldest Hadley, and gave it a quick shake. She used the excuse of accepting Ben's hand to extract her hand from Garrett's lingering grip.

"Aren't you leaving something out, Neisson?" Garrett asked in a voice almost as deep as Ian's.

Ian simply regarded him with a single raised blond eyebrow.

Ben leaned forward as if to make sure she didn't miss his cheeky smile. "We're family."

"Not yet," Ian grumbled.

"Soon enough," Ben shot back. To Jessie he said, "Our baby brother, Bodie, is engaged to his only sister, Caitlin."

Something Jessie already knew. What she didn't know was why Ian seemed less than pleased to have his future brother-in-law's family join them.

Ian asked Garrett, "You buying or selling?"

As curious as she was about the men's relationship, she was thankful for Ian redirecting the conversation away from the personal.

"Buying," Garrett answered. "Bodie keeps cherry-picking our best cows for his bucking bull breeding program, so we need more for our rough stock program."

"Plus we've had more than a few head go missing this summer. Easier to replace them than hunt them down."

Garrett shot his brother a look that caught Jessie's attention. The oldest Hadley definitely hadn't wanted that tidbit to get out. At least not to her and Ian.

Jessie wasn't terribly surprised. Ranchers were proud folk. One thing she'd had reinforced while investigating the rash of thefts in the ION territory was that ranchers, big or small, didn't want to be known for not being able to keep track of their livestock. They often didn't report the thefts, which made tracking and recovering the herds being transported across state lines nearly impossible—which was why Jessie was taking this current tack to catch the thieves.

"You might be in luck today." Ian tapped the auction schedule on his thigh.

"Hope so," Garrett said.

Ben asked, "What are you in the market for? Or is the auction barn a Neisson's idea of a hot date?"

Ian's eyes narrowed.

Jessie thought it best to interject, "I wanted to see what a livestock auction was like. Ian kindly offered to let me tag along with him here today."

Two sets of dark eyebrows shot up.

Ben said, "You actually wanted to see what a livestock auction was like?"

Jessie nodded as guilelessly as she could. "Absolutely."

The brothers exchanged a quick look. They either thought her a lunatic or a cowboy's dream girl.

Garrett's eyes narrowed slightly. "How do you two know each other? You're certainly not from around here."

"College," she answered quickly, not surprised in the least that two bucks such as these would be acquainted with the town's female population. "We're friends from college."

"Friends who have a lot of catching up to do, so . . ." Ian gave a vague gesture with his hand, but his *beat it* message was clear.

Both Hadleys nodded their understanding, but the speculative gleam still lit their gray eyes.

"It was a pleasure meeting you, Jessie," Garrett said. "Will you be at Liam and Amanda's engagement party? The way Thomas Wright puts on a shindig, anyone who is anyone around here will be there."

Anyone as in Grant Williams? Nothing like an open bar to aid a little subtle interrogation. Having recovered Ian's brother's fiancée Amanda Rodrigues's prized stallion and arrested the man who'd stolen it, an invitation to the upcoming party at the Wright Ranch had been a given. Obviously, Jessie had initially declined, but perhaps she needed to rethink attending the party.

She smiled brightly at the Hadley brothers. "I might."

Ian leaned forward to interject, "If she's still around."

A twisted part of her had her repeating, "I'm not going anywhere for a while." At this rate she'd end up with the words tattooed over her ribs.

The edges of Garrett's gray eyes crinkled with his smile. "Excellent. I'll see you then. Hopefully I'll see you around too."

Ben said, "If you get bored of this stick-in-the-mud, pop over to our place. I'll give you the grand tour."

Ian made a disparaging sound low in his throat.

Jessie ignored him and said her thanks but Garrett and Ben apparently took the growl as their cue to find seats elsewhere.

When the two men had moved to spots on a lower bench Jessie turned and asked Ian, "You don't like your future in-laws?"

"Let's just say there's history there."

"Like what?"

Ian shrugged as if it was nothing.

Peter said through the earpiece, "The sheriff is quoted as saying there was a longstanding feud between the two families."

She remembered reading that part of the sheriff's statement, but had dismissed it at the time after learning of Bodie Hadley and Caitlin Neisson's engagement. Now she realized she might have been too hasty.

"Like what?" she repeated.

"Like our grandfather raised us to believe the Hadleys were not good people because of something that happened between him and the Hadley boys' grandfather. But thanks to Caitlin, we finally discovered what had started the whole thing. And that was the end of it."

"A decades-long feud ended just like that?"

"Just like that."

"And the thing was . . . ?"

He shifted to look at her fully. "Nosey much, Special Agent Martin?"

"Occupational hazard." Unrepentant, she mimicked his shrug. "And please, call me Jessie."

His eyebrows twitched upward beneath the brim of his hat.

"There will be less chance of you accidentally outing me as a special agent if you get used to calling me Jessie all the time."

He didn't exactly look happy about the familiarity, or having to get used to calling her anything with any amount of frequency, but his quick nod let her know he agreed with her logic.

"So . . . the thing was?" she persisted.

He rolled his eyes and shifted back toward the auction corral below them. "Let's just say it involved a woman and definitely didn't warrant a longstanding feud that sucked in two subsequent generations."

"Sucked in how?"

"Are all your conversations cross-examinations?"

While she wanted to state the obvious, *FBI*, considering where they were, she defaulted to, "I did clock in this morning."

He stared into his coffee for a moment.

Looking for his patience? Or rethinking his willingness to work with her?

He sighed, this time one of acceptance. "Our fathers

competed for rodeo rough stock contracts, at least as much as my father was involved in the business." He took a sip of his coffee as if to wash away a bad memory. "Garrett is a year older than I am and Ben a year younger. And Bodie is close to Liam's age. We all went to school together, competing against each other in pretty much everything. And trust me, it was not a friendly competition."

"But now it's all good?"

He took another drink of his coffee. "I wouldn't say it's all good, but we're getting there."

"Enough to invite them to another engagement party?"

"Amanda is Caitlin's best friend, and with Caitlin about to marry into the Hadley clan, of course she wanted them invited."

Just then the auctioneer's voice came over the PA to announce the start of the auction, drawing Ian's attention.

Jessie was glad for the interruption, because as she absorbed what Ian had told her, two very uncomfortable, not to mention unprofessional, sensations bloomed in her chest. Her heart crimped for Ian being drawn into an adult's grudge as a child. But mostly she felt jealousy spreading through her. Jealous that he had a family who would maintain a feud for a member of the family without even knowing the cause. A family who were clearly dedicated to each other.

A family very different from her own.

She'd known being sent here to work this case would be difficult for her, but she'd never expected this. And she had no choice but to deal with it by locking the distracting emotions down and staying focused, because as she kept saying, *she was not going anywhere for a while.*

SHIT. JUST . . . shit.

Now he'd have an FBI agent attending his brother's engagement party at his family's home. A drop-dead gorgeous FBI agent everyone thought he was dating. He didn't doubt for a moment those in attendance here today would spread the news of his newly arrived college "friend." How she'd clung to his arm and smiled up at him. How he'd freed her sleek black hair from her jacket collar, his fingers sliding down the long ponytail as if they had a mind of their own. The silky feel of her hair was forever burned into his brain.

What was wrong with him?

It took everything in Ian not to crush the paper coffee cup in his hand. But the last thing he wanted to do was let Special Agent Martin—Jessie—know how much she affected him or how much he didn't want her at his brother's engagement party, or anywhere near his family. The way her brain seemed to work, she would undoubtedly interpret his refusal as guilt.

With her gaze on the Hereford cow and young calf just released into the auction corral, Jessie asked, "Will Grant Williams be at the engagement party?"

"Yes. Of course. He and his family. We've known the Williamses my entire life."

"So you can tell me about Mr. Williams?"

"What would you like to know?"

"Something other than the fact he once employed a certain murderous bull straw thief."

Memories of what Karl Fletcher had cost his family mixed with the coffee he'd drunk to form an acidic brew in his gut. The bitterness seeped into his tone. "Don't forget he was employed by my grandfather first."

She met his gaze, her green eyes steady. "Trust me, I haven't."

The acid turned toxic. "Do you honestly think my grandfather committed crimes with the man who stole from us, caused the death of my mother and my cousin, and nearly killed my sister?"

She looked away. "I wouldn't have asked for your help if I did."

The words were the right ones, but there was something in her tone that prickled the back of his neck. Why was he helping this woman?

Because he had to protect his family and his community by making sure the truth came out, that was why. And because, though he was loath to admit it, she had been there to help him when he'd needed her.

He set the suddenly unappealing coffee on the bench next to him. "Look, I don't believe for a second Grant would have hired Karl Fletcher if he had known Fletch was the ranch hand who'd disappeared the day Mom was injured. It was nearly ten years before the guy resurfaced."

"I won't know what to believe until I have a chance to talk to Mr. Williams."

"Then call him into the sheriff's station and formally talk

to him. Straight up ask him your questions, without all the lies and subterfuge."

She scoffed. "If only. You see, there's this funny thing about people involved in illegal activity. They generally don't freely admit to their wrongdoing. No matter how nicely they are asked."

"Having sat on the opposite side of an interrogation table, I have a hard time picturing you asking nicely."

She grinned at him as if he'd just told her she was the prettiest woman he'd ever seen.

She was, but that was beside the point. Desperately wanting her to change her mind about attending Liam and Amanda's party, he leaned forward and anchored his elbows on his knees again. "But you think Grant will tell you, a complete stranger he just met at an engagement party, that he has committed a crime?"

She laughed, the sound shockingly light for a woman he knew to be carrying a small handgun holstered beneath her leather jacket. He'd seen the holster peek from beneath her jacket when she'd climbed from his truck. He hadn't intentionally been looking at what might lie beneath her jacket, but the swell of her breasts beneath her white T-shirt drew his attention like a short lead line.

"Have a little faith, Ian. They let me do this for a reason."

By *this* he assumed she meant being an FBI special agent. He didn't doubt she could do her job, despite the fact she couldn't have been doing it very long.

"How old are you?"

She pulled her chin back. "Didn't your—" She cut herself off, but he knew what she'd almost said.

Yes, his mother had taught him to never ask a woman her age. She'd also taught him family was everything.

But so far, Special Agent Jessie Martin had helped his family and proven her worth as a law enforcement officer. She'd found Amanda's stallion and arrested the man who'd taken him faster than Ian had thought possible. That didn't mean he wanted her at his home, at an important family event, for the sole purpose of trying to get dirt on one of his grandfather's oldest friends.

Especially because she was the prettiest woman he'd ever seen. And he was finding it hard not to like her. Or to not think about those tempting lips of hers.

CHAPTER FOUR

A WEEK LATER Jessie was once again in the passenger seat of a ridiculously large truck. Only this time the blacked-out vehicle belonged to the local sheriff's department, and Peter was at the wheel, driving her to the engagement party of the second oldest grandson of Thomas Wright and their neighbor Amanda Rodrigues.

With the input of the sheriff, she and Peter had determined an unmarked sheriff's vehicle would draw less attention parked along the road outside of the Wright Ranch's security gate than the surveillance van they had used outside the auction barn. Arriving late, Peter would drop her off, then park within the ample two-thousand-foot range of the camera she'd worn today.

Just as on the day of Caitlin Neisson and Bodie Hadley's engagement party, when she'd delivered Amanda's recovered stallion, the tall, ornately scrolled and monogrammed wrought-iron gate stood wide open to allow the guests entrance without having to be buzzed through. And just like the previous engagement party, the drive leading to the main house that circled around a life-size bronze statue of a rearing horse was packed with various vehicles, mostly dually trucks.

It was clear from the number of vehicles present Thomas Wright hosted well-attended parties. Hopefully she'd have more success here than she had at the auction.

"There," Peter said, pointing at a white truck with Bar W stenciled on the side. Unless someone else was driving his truck, Grant Williams was indeed in attendance. While his ranch was named the Bar W, Grant Williams was the principle shareholder in S and R Genetics, the corporation his bucking bulls were owned by. Hopefully he didn't have a truck emblazoned with the S and R Genetics logo that he drove. There was only one way to find out.

Jessie's heart rate kicked up a notch. Game time.

Peter had barely stopped their truck before Jessie was hopping out and heading for the front walk. Running through the list of possible questions she would ask Mr. Williams, she didn't look back as Peter drove down the asphalt-paved drive toward the road. They had spent the majority of the past week in Bend where Karl Fletcher and his horse thief cohort were being held. Reinterviewing the men, she and Peter had attempted to learn more about the supposed record of the thefts beyond that it was being kept by one of the rich guys. Neither of them would cooperate further.

As she walked up the steps to the massive front door of the Wright Ranch main house, reminding her once again more of a resort lodge than a private home, Jessie touched her gold horseshoe necklace for luck and smoothed the silky material of her lightweight off-white pantsuit over her hips. She had to do something with her hands to stifle what had become the unfortunate habit of fiddling with the surveillance camera. Today they had hidden the tiny audiovisual device within an intricate brooch pinned to the broad, pointed lapel of her suit jacket.

Along with the flowy, wide-legged palazzo pants and kitten heels, the fitted jacket was as far from her normal work suit as could be. Especially with nothing but the small battery pack beneath the jacket. After she'd convinced him to add her undercover persona to the engagement party guest list, Ian had told her the party would be a casual affair here at the ranch.

But she wanted, needed, certain guests also attending Liam and Amanda's engagement party to focus on what she looked like instead of who, or more importantly, what she was—namely an FBI special agent with an agenda. Or why she was grilling them on their latest livestock acquisitions while standing next to Thomas Wright's grill. And she doubted she'd be that overdressed. Judging from the stunning main house with its bronze horse sculpture out front, Thomas Wright didn't exactly do casual.

Jessie raised her hand to knock but the big door swung open before her knuckles made contact. Ian stood in the doorway, having obviously been watching for her. He looked very polished in pressed dark-washed jeans, a crisp white button-down shirt, a tan suede western-style blazer, and matching cowboy boots. The only nod to casual she could discern was the lack of a cowboy hat. Her gaze caught on his thick, sun-bleached blond hair. Previously she'd only seen it curling from beneath his hat or smooshed flat to his head when he took his hat off. There was no denying the man had glorious hair. Not to mention he was handsome in that rugged cowboy way that both thrilled and annoyed her.

After he took a moment to look her up and down as well, his dark blue eyes inscrutable, he said, "Special Age—"

She held up a finger to stop him, flicking her gaze over his shoulder to see if anyone stood near enough behind him to have heard. The expansive entryway behind him appeared empty.

He inclined his head slightly in acknowledgment of his near slip. They had only talked briefly over the phone during the week and he had clearly slipped back into his habit of addressing her formally.

"Jessie," he amended his greeting.

With the memory of his muscular thigh pressed against hers when they were seated in the auction barn seared into her brain, formality wouldn't be such a bad thing between them, but it wouldn't serve her purpose here today. So she smiled brightly and infused warmth into her voice. "Ian."

He stepped aside to allow her to enter. "I was beginning to think you'd changed your mind about coming."

Was that hope in his tone?

"Of course not." She stepped past him, all too aware of his gaze on her and the smell of his spicy aftershave. The scent was nothing unusual, but the way it invaded her senses and drew her in was very new. Why was the scent so appealing on him?

Needing to put more distance between them, she strode into the foyer, then paused for a moment to take in the rustic grandeur that was the Wright Ranch main house.

She'd known from the list of assets in the file they had on Thomas Wright that the house was well over ten thousand square feet, but seeing the numbers on paper wasn't the same as seeing the interior of the place in person. With slate tile and vaulted, timber-framed ceilings, the home was a showplace of the western lodge style of construction and decorating.

Ian closed the big front door with a deceptively soft click and moved beside her, invading her space with his scent, size, and sheer presence.

"The party is out back." His gaze dropped to the pointed toe, kitten-heeled shoes that perfectly matched her suit. "On the patio. We can go through the breakfast nook." Meeting her gaze again with an amused glint in his eyes, he gestured toward a wide doorway where she could see a wall of windows in a "nook" large enough for a rough-hewn table with ten matching chairs.

Apparently, everything about the Wright Ranch was supersize.

She lifted her chin, still confident in her clothing choice. "Lead the way," she said, preferring to enter the gathering without him watching her from behind.

He scoffed. "Ladies first."

Damn cowboys. She stifled a sigh and pasted on a smile before proceeding toward the back of the big house. She only had the opportunity to glance down the two long hallways branching off from the main entrance foyer, which she guessed led to opposite wings of the house. Down which hall did Thomas Wright's home office lie? Could she even dare to hope there would be a flash drive or printout boldly labeled *Rustling Operation* sitting atop the desk? She suppressed a snort. She would never be so lucky. Their best hope was still someone slipping up enough for them to get their warrant.

Jessie hesitated after entering the breakfast "nook," momentarily boggled by the size and beauty of the attached gourmet kitchen. It was a symphony of stone, granite, and steel with ample room for the catering crew, who were dressed in black slacks, white shirts, and narrow black ties and at work filling champagne glasses and platters of canapés and salmon rolls. Not exactly the typical rodeo rough stock ranch fare.

But Thomas Wright and the Neissons were not typical ranchers. With world-class bucking bulls and other rodeo rough stock, they had built a dynasty. The question that continued to niggle at her was *how.*

She could actually feel Ian hovering behind her, waiting. His presence enveloped her. He might not be part of a typical ranching family, but he was, without a doubt, a typical cowboy. *Ladies first.* She mentally rolled her eyes.

He must have caught the gaze of one of the servers, because the young woman's face erupted with eagerness to please and she hurried toward them with two full champagne glasses. Ian stepped forward and took them from her with a rumbling "thank you" that had the girl's face flaming.

Oh, to be that young again.

She met Ian's gaze as she took the glass from him, fully

expecting to see the gleam of a man who knew full well the effect he had on women, but what she saw gave her pause. Caution. Wariness. A hint of fear?

Ian Neisson was afraid of her? Or of what she might discover?

As her hand closed around the delicate crystal champagne flute, her fingers brushing against his with a jolt of electricity, Jessie realized something very important. She seriously needed to stop thinking of him as just a cowboy looking to breach the walls she'd spent the last ten years building and instead think of him only as a very well-connected, very wealthy rancher who potentially had something to hide.

She smiled at him, working hard to make the smile reach her eyes, and cooed, "Thank you, Ian. I need this." She saluted him with the champagne glass then raised it to her lips, continuing to watch him over the rim.

His eyes narrowed, clearly not buying her need for champagne, which only proved he didn't know her very well. "You're welcome." He arched a light blond eyebrow and indicated the French doors standing open to a large, crowded patio. "Shall we?"

In her ear Peter said, "I'm in position and reception is good. Go get 'em, tiger."

She really wished he'd stop saying *go get 'em, tiger*. It made her feel like she was twelve again being blithely sent off to do what a parent should have done. Nonetheless she casually slipped a hand beneath her hair and tapped an acknowledgment on the earpiece.

Draining most of her champagne in one go because, well, *cowboys*, Jessie walked ahead of Ian through the open French doors. He paused to retrieve a dark brown cowboy hat from atop the granite breakfast bar separating the kitchen from the breakfast nook. She waited for him to settle the hat atop his head, mashing down all that glorious blond hair, before stepping out into the pleasantly warm, early evening air.

Just like the house, the patio was a huge space comprised of stamped, tinted concrete that matched the seemingly endless high desert landscape visible beyond the lush, irrigated lawn and pasture land surrounding the main house and outbuildings. Rimming the patio were stone-encased outdoor beer taps, grills, sinks, and linen-covered serving tables set up and manned by the catering staff. Compared to what she'd grown up with, the sight was nothing short of heavenly, aside from the fact the patio was filled to the brim with cowboys and a few women who undoubtedly loved them.

And, just like the auction barn, they were all looking at her.

Her and Ian, she amended as she felt his big, warm hand settle on the small of her back, gently urging her forward. It wasn't until then that she realized she'd stopped short in her tracks.

Amanda Rodrigues, wearing a pretty peach sundress, separated herself from a group of very handsome men by the beer taps and hurried toward them.

Amanda opened her mouth, but before she could say anything, Ian stepped forward and cut her off.

"Amanda, you remember my friend from college, Jessie Martin." Clearly he'd been afraid she'd out Jessie as being a federal agent.

Amanda huffed. "Yes, of course I remember Jessie. I'm so glad you could make it today."

Jessie leaned toward Ian and spoke softly, "I texted Amanda earlier and made sure she was okay with me coming and under what circumstances."

Amanda gave Ian a *duh* look born of a lifetime of familiarity.

Ian muttered, "Of course you did."

Amanda extended her hand and Jessie clasped Amanda's hand in hers, thinking no one could look as amazing as Amanda did in the flowy sundress similar to the yellow floral dress she'd worn to Caitlin Neisson's engagement party. Jessie had inadvertently interrupted those festivities, at least for Amanda and Liam, with the return of the stolen stallion. "I wouldn't have missed it for the world. Thank you so much for inviting me."

Amanda squeezed Jessie's hand before releasing her. "Do you remember telling me my future was going to be bright?"

Jessie did. Amanda had told her that Whiskey Throttle, the stallion Jessie had recovered, represented Amanda's future. Knowing a little about quality horseflesh, Jessie had told Amanda her future would be bright then.

Amanda looked back over her shoulder at Liam, the second oldest Neisson sibling, standing in the center of the patio talking to an older gentleman who bore a slight resemblance to Amanda. The sigh she released was one of pure happiness. "Now it looks like I'm going to need shades."

Jessie's throat tightened unexpectedly at the corny song reference. Why was she getting emotional over two people she barely knew? From what she had learned about the family, Liam was the most volatile of the Neisson siblings. But the look on Amanda's face was one of pure bliss.

Maybe having grown up on a ranch that shared a fence line with the Wright Ranch and being best friends with the lone Neisson girl had given Amanda a different perspective of Liam. Though not as tall or as commanding a presence as Ian, Liam was undeniably gorgeous in a big, muscly farm boy kind of way. And the look he sent back at Amanda made it clear he absolutely adored the pretty brunette. He briefly said something to the man he'd been talking to, who perhaps was Amanda's uncle, and moved toward them as if Amanda had tugged on his lead line.

He, too, extended a hand toward Jessie, which she accepted for a quick shake. "Really glad you could make it . . . Jessie." The informal address didn't seem to roll off his tongue as easily as it had for his new fiancée, and the look he sent Ian was definitely one of caution.

Did he also know there was something to hide here at the Wright Ranch?

Ian leaned down and totally derailed Jessie's thoughts by saying in her ear, "Let me introduce you around."

She had to blink to focus, but could tell by his tone that he meant Grant Williams. Fine. Good, actually. The sooner she questioned Mr. Williams the sooner she could be out of here. She needed to get out of here.

Jessie tilted away from Ian, for sanity's sake, and said, "Yes, that would be great." To Liam and Amanda, she said, "Thank you, again, for allowing me to attend. And please accept my sincerest congratulations."

"Of course. And thank *you*," Amanda said, her smile wide.

Ian surprised Jessie by taking her hand, his palm hot and rough against hers, and leading her through the crowd toward a cluster of older gentlemen who were the epitome of rich ranchers. All high-end hats, boots, and suede and leather western-cut blazers.

Garrett and Ben Hadley stepped into her and Ian's path.

"You made it!" Ben spread his arms as if inviting her in for a hug.

Not freakin' likely. While remaining rooted to her spot, Jessie sent him what she hoped was a delighted smile. "I did!"

Ian moved a fraction closer to her.

Garrett's sharp gray gaze moved between Jessie and Ian before settling on her. "Did you enjoy the auction?"

"Immensely," she said on a sigh of feigned bliss. "But Ian and I were too busy catching up for him to manage any bidding." She smiled up at Ian and bumped her shoulder against his biceps.

He smiled back, but the corners of his mouth looked tight.

Garrett said, "The invitation to tour the Hadley Cattle Company still stands."

She had to give him points for not being easily deterred.

Ben's grin widened. "Yeah. The *grand* tour."

Jessie clenched her back teeth together to hold her smile in place and commenced counting to ten.

Before she reached the number four a beautiful woman with long blond hair and vivid blue eyes shoved her way between the Hadleys. Caitlin Neisson.

"Stop, you two," Caitlin said. "Can't you see she's with Ian? And you know darn well that if she needs anything, he'll see to it." To Jessie she said, "Pay these Rodeo Romeos no mind." She gave her two soon-to-be brothers-in-law an affectionate squeeze on the shoulders then shooed them on their way with a gentle shove. She stuck out her hand to Jessie. "Hi. I'm Caitlin Neisson."

Jessie did her best to strip any sign of recognition from her expression and shook the younger woman's hand. "Jessie Martin. Nice to finally meet you, Caitlin. Ian has told me all about you." He hadn't, but Jessie still felt like she knew Caitlin after extensively questioning the man who'd tried, repeatedly, to kill her. The same murderous bull straw thief employed first by Thomas Wright then by Grant Williams— right before his arrest.

Caitlin beamed at her oldest brother. "Probably all the bad stuff."

Ian hitched his thumbs in the front pockets of his jeans. "Nope. That would have taken too long."

Caitlin rolled her eyes. "Har, har, Ian. And because I know there's no way I'm going to count on him to tell us all about you, I'm afraid you'll have to do it."

Caitlin moved to take Jessie's arm, probably to lead her away, but Ian slipped an arm around her waist and pulled her close to his side.

Jessie's brain immediately left the building. Her body flushed hot and her breathing hitched.

To his sister, Ian said, "Let me introduce her to some people first."

Caitlin dropped her outstretched hands, her smile broadening. "Okay." She met Jessie's gaze. "Later?"

Thankfully, Jessie regained her ability to speak in time to answer, "Absolutely."

As soon as Caitlin left to join a different group of people chatting, Ian loosened his hold and said, "Sorry about that."

"No problem," Jessie said through the tightness in her throat as Ian started to guide her forward again. She told herself her throat had closed up because he was still very close to her, but she knew deep down it was from a longing she'd buried a long time ago and wanted desperately to stay buried.

To make that happen, she forced herself to focus on the group of men Ian was leading her toward.

Though she had studied a photo of Grant Williams she and Peter had acquired from the DMV, picking Mr. Williams out at a glance from the group of similarly aged ranchers would have taken her a long minute. Luckily for her, she had Ian, who steered her toward one gentleman in particular. The similarities to the picture hit her as they drew near.

Grant Williams appeared shorter than the five foot ten

inches listed on his driver's license, and it had definitely been a few years since he'd weighed in at one ninety-five. He also now sported a snowy white goatee.

Peter said softly into the earpiece, "That's our man."

Jessie didn't feel the need to acknowledge the obvious.

Ian stopped next to Mr. Williams, placing a hand on the man's shoulder.

The move was unnecessary. All eyes in the group were already on her and Ian. The looks of eager anticipation made it clear they expected Ian to introduce them to his new lady love. Not great for her equilibrium, but not a bad thing at all for gaining their trust.

But could she trust Ian to lie to people he was reputed to be devoted to?

IAN'S RESOLVE WAVERED the moment his hand settled on the shoulder of one of his grandfather's oldest friends. Grant Williams had been a fixture in Ian's life, always there to lend a hand or send over a crew when needed. How could he look into the still-sharp brown eyes of a man he knew trusted him without question and lie to him?

But what choice did he have? The black-haired, green-eyed beauty at his side wasn't simply local law enforcement looking into a couple of thefts. She was FBI, for god's sake, intent on busting a multimillion-dollar modern cattle rustling ring. Something that would benefit them all. Even the Hadleys had suffered losses.

Ian wanted to help. He had to help. He just wasn't certain he could.

Especially with the way those green eyes of hers sparkled up at him and how the accidental graze of her silky, stick-straight black hair on the back of his hand sent his heart racing.

If he weren't careful, he'd forget this was all pretend.

CHAPTER FIVE

I AN PULLED HIS gaze from Special Agent Martin's mesmerizing green eyes and, after giving one last quick squeeze, he released Grant Williams's shoulder. His feelings for either one didn't matter. The only thing that mattered was his family. And he would do what he had to do to protect them.

Including lying like a dog.

"Gentlemen." He glanced around the group of neighbors and longtime family friends. "I'd like you to meet a very good friend of mine from college, Jessie Martin." He placed a hand on Jessie's back again, inadvertently trapping her glorious black hair beneath his palm and further torturing himself, to ease her forward. Then he proceeded to introduce her to the group of older men, saving Grant for last.

She shook hands with them all, charming them with a seemingly genuine combination of friendliness and real, focused interest in each man as she greeted them.

Or she was simply searching her memory for each man's list of possible priors.

Either way, they all sent Ian glowing looks of approval. It was enough to make the champagne he'd just drunk turn sour in his stomach. Then he made it worse by wondering if there was some man out there somewhere who actually did get to bask in the approval of other men by having made her his own. Her partner, Special Agent Peter Beck?

No. Ian rejected the thought as soon as he had it. The two hadn't given off the vibe of a romantic couple. But what did he know of FBI vibes?

He did know something about bull-headedness, though, and Special Agent Jessica Martin vibed that in spades, evident by the way she held on to Grant's hand after shaking it, unlike the other men.

Wanting this over as quickly as possible by allowing her to ask Grant the questions she felt so compelled to ask, Ian dropped his hand from her back and did his best to engage the other ranchers in idle chit-chat. He kept an ear open to the conversation Jessie was having with Grant, though.

As he was fielding questions about how he was handling Liam's moving of the Wright Ranch's bucking bronc breeding and training program over to Amanda's neighboring Sky High Ranch, he heard Jessie work her way from how close Grant's ranch was located to the Wright Ranch to whether or not Grant and Thomas ever hired the same ranch hands. She already knew that Grant had unknowingly hired Karl Fletcher, the hand who had stolen bull straws and god only knew what else from Ian's grandfather then released their champion bucking bull to trample Ian's mother when she'd caught him in the act. Fletch had also tried to kill his sister, Caitlin, in a similar fashion, thinking she could identify him, too, because she'd been with their mother that fateful day. As if that wasn't enough, Fletch was additionally indirectly responsible for their cousin Charlie's death.

Thanks to Caitlin's fiancé, Bodie Hadley, Fletch was in custody. But what lies had he told the federal agents? He could have implicated any number of people in order to save his own hide.

Ian's temper flared and he couldn't help flinching slightly when Jessie snaked an arm around his as if she'd done it a thousand times. But her pulling him closer also served to bring him into her and Grant's conversation.

"Ian was sweet enough to take me to the auction barn last weekend. I wanted to see firsthand how he buys his steers at auction."

Grant perked up. "Oh?" The man did love cattle. Big, mean bucking bulls like his bull, Kraken, in particular, but he'd happily talk steers or roping calves too. Which was why he and Ian's grandfather had been such good friends for so long.

Grant asked, "Was he successful?"

"Sadly, no," Jessie said. "I suppose we weren't as focused on the auction offerings as we should have been." Again with the flirty smile, this time aimed squarely at Ian.

His gut clenched with the impact. The woman was ruthless.

She returned her attention to Grant. "But I'd really like to try out my bidding gesture at least once." She raised a hand high, her palm cupped slightly, and gave what looked more like a queenly wave than an auction bid.

Grant threw back his head and laughed. A sound from Ian's childhood. "I'm sure Ian can find time to take you again. If not, you come see me and I'll take you." The old bastard winked right at Ian.

Ian sent him a smile that was mostly snarl. He couldn't help it. What was with these guys? It wasn't as if there was a shortage of pretty women in Pineville. Granted, none of them showed up in runway-worthy pantsuits, showing off enough cleavage to rob a man of spit for a year. But still.

The same member of the catering staff who'd brought them their first glass of champagne in the kitchen—he was pretty sure her name was Kylie and that she raced barrels like Amanda—stepped up to their group. She held a full tray of filled champagne glasses, offering to exchange for their empties. Ian hadn't even realized he'd downed the entire contents of his first glass.

He had the overwhelming urge to keep the two he'd taken for himself, but instead handed one to Jessie after she'd placed her empty glass on the tray.

Grant hoisted his half-filled glass of bourbon and winked in an apparent indication he was good on the refreshments front.

As soon as Kylie moved away, his two younger brothers jostled to take her place, their blue eyes bright with mischief. Would they ever grow up?

Drew managed to get closest first. "Ian, my man. I know you've never been the sort to kiss and tell . . . but dude, you've been holding out on us."

Alec angled his shoulder in front of Drew. "Yeah, Ian. Introduce us to your friend." His gaze traveled over Jessie as if she were a championship buckle in heels.

Ian had been afraid of this. He hadn't brought a woman home to the ranch for a very long time. His focus had been entirely on the ranch and his family. Grandfather had come to rely on him to handle the day-to-day running of the ranch even more than his father relied on him to ride herd on his siblings. He didn't need the aggravation of a woman in his life. But he didn't exactly have much of a choice at the moment.

Filling his lungs with a hopefully calming breath, he let it out slowly before meeting Jessie's gaze. It was clear she knew darn well the position she'd put him in with his family, and the upward twitch of one of her midnight brows said she wasn't the least contrite about it.

While he was tempted to either down his champagne in one go or turn on his boot heel and simply leave, instead he said, "Jessie, meet my two youngest siblings, Andrew—"

"Call me Drew." He offered his hand. Jessie shifted her champagne glass to her other hand so she could shake it.

"And Alec. The baby," Ian added purposefully. Ever since Alec had successfully started riding bulls competitively, the kid had been acting too big for his britches.

Grant snorted a laugh.

Alec threw him a glare before giving a quick tug on the brim of his cowboy hat then offering his hand. "Ma'am."

Jessie's lips pressed together briefly before she smiled and shook Alec's hand too.

Giving her hand a little too enthusiastic of a shake, Alec said, "You have no idea how glad we are to see you here. Ian was starting to give us a bad name."

Both of Jessie's brows went up. "Oh? How so?"

Drew said, "All work and absolutely no play . . ."

"Ah." Her smile widened.

Not liking where this was going, Ian said, "All right, you two. That's enough."

Drew persisted, "If he gets too dull for you, I am totally free to help you with any and all your needs."

Now my brothers are sounding like the Hadley boys, Ian thought sourly. Since Caitlin and Bodie had thawed the frost between the two families, they had been interacting more. Maybe too much.

Alec elbowed his brother. "Don't you have some of that fancy college homework to do?"

"Don't you have dirt to eat?" Drew countered.

Grant cleared his throat, drawing everyone's attention. "I was the one talking to the pretty lady. Why don't you two go pester some of the other guests?"

"Yes, sir," the boys said in unison, tipping their hats before leaving.

Jessie asked, "Homework and dirt?"

Ian supplied, "Drew is attending the state university and Alec is trying his hand at competitive bull riding."

Jessie nodded, turning to gaze toward the bull barn. "Makes sense."

Grant said solemnly, "Not really."

Her dark winged brows grew together, and Ian could tell the moment when she drew the correlation between Alec climbing on the back of a bull and their family history.

Her smile disappeared and she met Ian's gaze. "How do

you feel about that?"

Always the interrogator. But she wouldn't have to be a graduate of Quantico to figure it out, so he told her the truth. "Bull riding definitely wouldn't be the first choice of career for anyone in my family, but he's going about it the right way, thanks to Caitlin, and through her, Bodie Hadley." Nothing like a former champion bull rider who knew exactly how badly things could go in the arena to mentor Alec.

"Amen," Grant concurred. "As nerve-racking as it is, I'm looking forward to watching the boy ride at next weekend's rodeo. I'll even do my business in the grandstands if I have to."

Jessie lit up. "Do business? What kind?"

Grant looked at her for a moment as if she'd asked him boxers or briefs. "Well . . ."

A heavy hand clapped down on Ian's shoulder. He turned to find his father and grandfather standing behind him, wearing expressions of curious expectation. Great. Just great.

In his trademark deep, gruff voice, his grandfather said, "A rumor has been swirling around that my eldest grandson finally brought a girl home. But now I see how mistaken the gossips were. This is no girl—this is a stunning young woman. Introduce us, Ian." Not a request, but rather a command.

Suddenly Ian's mouth felt full of old straw. It was one thing to tell his neighbors, future family by marriage, and his siblings that Special Agent Martin was an old friend from college. But having to look either his father or his grandfather in the eye and lie to them would be worse than being trampled by a bull himself.

"IT'S GO TIME," Peter whispered excitedly in her ear.

Jessie barely heard him, instead intently watching the color leech from Ian Neisson's face after his grandfather, the famed Thomas Wright himself, requested an introduction for himself and Ian's father. She itched to stick out her hand and do it herself. To take pity on Ian.

Very unprofessional.

So she pasted on what she hoped would be a sweet, patient smile and waited for Ian to swallow his guilt, or fear, or whatever it was he was grappling with and introduce her to Douglas Neisson and Thomas Wright.

Being a true cowboy, Ian found his grit and settled one big, hot hand on her lower back and used the one holding his champagne—a very incongruent sight, she realized belatedly—to gesture between her and the older gentlemen.

"Grandfather, Dad, I'd like you to meet Jessie Martin. Jessie, meet Thomas Wright and Douglas Neisson."

She accepted Thomas's hand, surprised by how work roughened it was against her palm. "Sir."

Then she shook Douglas's hand, unconsciously searching his gaze for the legendary sorrow he reputedly struggled with since his wife's injury and ultimate death. And while she was probably being fanciful, she swore she could see his pain clouding his eyes like a cataract on his soul.

She swallowed hard and repeated, "Sir."

Ian's hand dropped away from her back and she strangely missed the contact. Probably for its warmth. With the late summer sun sliding behind the Cascade Mountains, the temperature was beginning to drop. At least, that's what she told herself.

While Thomas Wright considered her with the trademark shrewdness of a very successful man, Douglas Neisson smiled at her with a disarming genuineness. Jessie instantly liked him, something she wasn't supposed to feel in her line of work.

Douglas said, "I hear you know my Ian from college."

"That's correct, sir."

"Where do you hail from originally?"

"Colorado." Not true. But claiming to be from anywhere within the ION territory ran the risk of one or more of the investigation's principle suspects being familiar with who owned what.

Her family still lived on the Nevada cattle ranch she'd grown up on—a truth she was not ready to confide. She could get away with using her real name because her mother had taken her stepfather's name, but neither had been interested in him adopting her. For good measure she added, "A suburb outside of Denver. I've never even stepped onto a ranch before." She met Ian's gaze, but couldn't gauge what he did or didn't believe.

Thomas said, "But you came to Oregon to attend college?"

"Yes, sir." Not true. "I wanted a change of scenery." Very true. And the University of Southern California, in the heart of Los Angeles, was as much of a change as she could afford.

Douglas asked, "What did you study in school?"

"Law." Another truth. The more truths that could be worked into an undercover story, the better.

Grant said, "So you're a lawyer?" He sounded more amazed than worried.

"Sort of." She winked.

His chuckle was deep and a little knowing.

The patriarch of the Wright Ranch's gaze flitted over her fitted and low-cut suit and delicate, pointy-toed shoes. "I heard you were in town auditing the sheriff's books. I wasn't aware that accounting was part of a lawyer's job description."

No wonder Ian could spot an interrogation. He'd grown up with a master interrogator who didn't miss much. "I'm a forensic accounting lawyer, contracted by the state." Only sort of true, because she worked for the FBI. But she had a contact in the state's finance department who would vouch for her supposed employment.

Redirecting the conversation, Jessie said, "I'm so looking forward to seeing a rodeo." Big fat lie. She slid a glance at Ian, who was watching her closely. "Though I freely admit I mostly want an excuse to spend an afternoon with a certain cowboy."

She watched his chest expand with a deep breath. In relief or to contain his anger for her going down the *more than friends* road? It hadn't been in her plan, but it was easier than fighting the mood of the room, so to speak.

"Lucky cowboy," Douglas said, and Jessie looked back at Ian's father in time to see his grin widen in paternal pride.

Next to her she heard Ian expel the air he'd drawn in. Yep, he'd been working to contain his anger. His grandfather was still looking at her like he was trying to decide something.

She met his flinty blue gaze and didn't waver.

Thomas asked, "How long will you be visiting Pineville, Miss Martin?"

She started to say that she wasn't sure but Ian spoke first. "Not long."

"Then you should stay here, at the ranch. We certainly have room in the main house, or I'm sure Ian would be happy to clear his saddles out of the guest room in the ranch manager's house."

Through the earpiece Peter softly said, "Perfect chance for you to have a casual look-see at the ranch manager's office."

The ranch manager being Ian.

Jessie's breath caught in her throat.

"Yes. I'd be happy to do that," Ian surprised her by saying.

Peter said, "Hmm. Maybe the good stuff is in the main house."

By good stuff Jessie assumed Peter meant the mystical, magical flash drive or whatever Karl Fletcher had said contained a record of the thefts. Or at the very least records pertaining to Thomas Wright's hiring and stock purchasing. Only a little casual, still-admissible-in-court snooping would tell. Much riskier than simply eavesdropping or steering a few conversations in the right direction, but hopefully it would lead to a far speedier resolution.

She looked between the men. "You are all so kind. While nice, the Pineville Motel sure isn't this." She gestured toward the incredible vista beyond the patio, with the setting sun having just dipped below the snowcapped peaks of the Central Oregon Cascades and throwing them into silhouettes, the sky blazing red behind them.

"Then it's decided," Thomas said, his expression settling into one of self-satisfaction. To Ian he said, "Make sure you take her out for at least one ride around the ranch. The view from the south pasture is not to be missed. You can also check on the steers out there while you're at it. They're contracted for this weekend's rodeo."

"But there's no rush," Douglas interjected.

Thomas nodded in agreement. "Certainly. Absolutely no rush."

Both older men smiled encouragingly at Jessie and Ian. They weren't even trying to disguise their attempt at matchmaking.

Douglas said, "Ian, why don't you take Jessie over to the food table? You two can get something to eat before the younger boys devour everything."

"Yes, sir."

Ian's warm fingers took hold of her elbow as Jessie glanced at Grant. He'd angled himself back toward the group of men he'd been speaking with when she and Ian had first approached him and rejoined their conversation. She had failed to learn anything useful, save for the fact he'd be doing business at next weekend's rodeo, which actually might prove beneficial. While it had been well over a decade since she'd attended a rodeo, she'd definitely go to one now for a chance to find out what Grant might be up to.

Directing her attention to Thomas and Douglas she said, "It was a pleasure to meet you. Thank you so much for being so welcoming to me."

Thomas nodded. "I look forward to getting to know you better."

"Same."

It might have been Jessie's imagination, but it seemed as though Ian's grip tightened ever so slightly before urging her forward.

Though eating was the last thing Jessie was interested in at the moment, she allowed Ian to lead her toward the linen-draped table manned by two pretty female members of the catering crew. And sure enough, Alec and Drew, as well as two cowboys Jessie didn't know, were posted in front, piling their plates with delicious-smelling barbecue riblets, chilled giant prawns, and spicy chicken wings. They were also flirting away with the young women. Apparently the Hadleys weren't the only Rodeo Romeos here today.

Ian said, "Make a hole, boys."

All four of them immediately stepped to the side. There was no doubting how much respect Ian was afforded.

When they saw her at Ian's side, one of the cowboys Jessie didn't know looked to Alec and stage-whispered, "Is that her? Holy crap. You weren't kidding."

"Right?" Alec nodded his agreement.

That heavy sigh emanated from Ian again. She was starting to think of it as his trademark noise.

The cowboy set his overflowing plate down, wiped his hand on his jeans then stuck it out to her. "Name's Danny Kline, ma'am."

She shook his hand. "Pleasure to meet you. I'm Jessie Martin."

The other man followed suit. "Cabe McBride."

Jessie also shook his hand. "Pleasure."

"These two yahoos keep Bodie alive over at the Hadley spread," Drew said.

Cabe, who appeared to be the younger of the two, amended, "We wrangle Bodie's rodeo bucking bulls for him."

Alec laughed. "Like Drew said, you keep Bodie alive."

"Let the lady get some food," Ian grumbled.

They immediately moved another step back, allowing Jessie to take a plate for the food she didn't want.

Behind her she heard Danny say, "Man, Ian, you sure took your sweet time, but when you finally got around to it, you scored a beauty."

"She's a friend," Ian replied softly.

"Best get busy changing that."

Ian muttered something that might have been a thanks, or it could very well have been an expletive.

Jessie told herself the tightness building in her chest was because she found Ian's family's matchmaking attempts appalling. He was a grown man, perfectly capable of tending to his own romantic needs. Like her, he simply appeared uninclined to do so.

But a little voice coming from the part of her that she'd kept buried, deep down inside of her, for a very long time whispered that her chest—namely her heart—was being squeezed tight because she was envious. What would having a family and friends like these people have been like? Knowing someone always had her back and would help her through difficult times?

She brushed off the thought and helped herself to prawns for appearances' sake. Not feeling so alone would be equal to having a unicorn show up in her nonexistent barn. She was better off sticking to the strictly professional relationships she had with her fellow law enforcement members.

As if on cue, Peter said, "Mmm, shrimp. Any chance you can get a doggy bag?"

CHAPTER SIX

I AN SAT IN his truck in front of room 107 at the Pineville Motel, waiting for the digital clock on the dash to click over to 8:30 a.m. Special Agent Jessie Martin had agreed to allow him to pick her up and move her and her things to the Wright Ranch at nine, but he'd purposely arrived early. He'd parked next to the black, unmarked sheriff's pickup truck the two federal agents had borrowed. The vehicle was a stark reminder of what his life had become and turned his morning's coffee sour, adding to the acid that had been churning in his stomach since Liam and Amanda's engagement party the evening before.

He'd spent the night vacillating between anger from being manipulated and used, and just plain freaked out over being drawn so deeply into something he couldn't control. His offer to help the law enforcement track down the thieves responsible for stealing livestock from honest ranchers in the area, which he now knew included his sister's future in-laws, was rapidly spiraling into something he might not be able to extract himself or his family from.

Last night at the engagement party after Grandfather invited her to stay at the ranch, Ian had grasped for at least a little control back by offering to have Special Agent Martin stay in the ranch manager's house—his house—rather than the main house for one reason, and one reason only. To better keep an eye on her.

He had no idea what lengths she would go to try to find dirt on his grandfather. While he believed in his bones there was simply no dirt to be found, just the idea of her snooping around the main house deeply offended him.

To be fair, he'd insisted on picking her and her stuff up from the motel this morning in order to do a little snooping of his own. And he planned to knock on her door a half an hour early in the hopes she wouldn't be entirely ready to go yet, and while she finished packing, he would have a casual look-see. He had been itching to see what the two agents have been up to since their arrival, and Special Agent Martin accepting his grandfather's invitation had made him feel downright rashy.

He'd intended to expend the resulting excess energy on cleaning his spare room because, as his grandfather had said, Ian had filled the space with the things he liked to do himself, like oil his saddle, repair whatever tack he'd noticed needed it, and there was even the transmission to one of the ATVs that he'd been tinkering with for far too long.

Thankfully the tasks all allowed him to turn off his brain for a while, something he'd really needed lately. But he'd ultimately decided to leave everything as it was. Perhaps the smell of horse and motor oil would hasten the agent's departure.

Then he'd finally be able to get the image of the plunging neckline of her white pantsuit out of his brain and effectively squash his family's ridiculous attempts at match-making.

Ian checked the time again. 8:32 a.m. His jaw set, he grabbed his cowboy hat from the seat next to him and climbed out of his truck.

The curtains on the lone window belonging to room 107 were drawn, blocking out the morning sun and prying eyes. Ian settled his hat on his head, wishing he could settle the churning in his gut as easily. But he had literally grabbed more than one bull by the horns, so he could handle one federal agent.

He raised his hand to knock on the red-painted motel room door, but the door swung inward before he made contact. Special Agent Martin stood in the doorway, wearing a black T-shirt, faded jeans, and her well-worn cowboy boots. With her long black hair in a single braid down her back, the thought that she looked more like a woman who'd grown up on a ranch than some random suburb flashed through his brain.

He was seized by the need to find out. Simply to better protect his family, not because he harbored any interest in Jessie Martin.

He pulled his hat off his head. "Special Agent Martin."

"*Jessie*," she corrected. "You have to get used to calling me Jessie."

He dipped his chin in acknowledgment. "Jessie. Good morning."

"Good morning, Ian." She grinned at him, her beauty

ratcheting up yet another notch with her amusement.

Ian's mouth went dry and his stomach tightened. Yeah. Not interested at all.

She opened the door wider. "'Bout time you got out of your truck and came to the door. We were beginning to think you were talking yourself out of helping."

At her mention of "we" Ian looked over her shoulder into the room, spotting Special Agent Beck seated at a table covered with stacks of files and papers, an open laptop in front of him.

Frowning, Ian glanced at the curtain-shrouded window and the peephole in the door. "You were watching?"

Stepping aside so he could enter, Jessie said, "Of course."

"We're always watching," Beck added with a smirk but his focus remained on the computer screen as he typed.

The adjoining doors between room 107 and 108 stood open.

Ian hadn't considered the possibility that Beck might be working in the room Jessie had said she'd been staying in. He knew they had set up an office, of sorts, at the sheriff's station, but they clearly had been working out of the hotel as well.

Moving toward the table as Jessie closed the door, Ian held his hat between his hands and tried his best to strike a casual stance. "I got here early, so I was trying to kill time."

Beck looked pointedly at his watch. "Not very well."

Having come to their door a full half hour early, Ian couldn't think of anything else to say other than simply, "Sorry."

Jessie waved him off. "It's fine. I'm ready to go. I just have to grab my toiletry bag out of the bathroom. You can go ahead and take the suitcase out to your truck." As she headed toward the bathroom Jessie pointed to a large, silver hard-sided wheeled suitcase standing upright next to the lone bed in the room, the suitcase's pull handle already raised and waiting. Atop the bed sat an equally large black duffel bag and an ample, tote-style dark brown purse. So much for catching her before she'd finished packing. The woman was organized.

Ian hesitated before doing as he'd been told, lingering by the table and attempting to scan what documents he could. There seemed to be a combination of financial statements generated by various banks and typed interview notes.

Without looking up from the laptop screen or pausing his typing, Beck said, "We already gave you all the paper-work we wanted you to see, Mr. Neisson."

He said it like they still considered him more of a suspect than an ally. Did they honestly think he would allow them onto the Wright Ranch if his family had something to hide? It took a conscious effort not to crush the brim of his hat in his hands. He was not used to being questioned. He didn't like it.

"Have you had a chance to go over the purchase records we sent you?" Jessie said as she emerged from the bathroom, having obviously heard her partner. She had a nondescript black toiletry bag in her hands.

Ian was struck by how different it was from his sister's toiletry bag, which was a pink, floral, girly thing. Though

Jessie wore minimal makeup, she hadn't struck him as the type to eschew girly things. Especially after seeing her in that suit she'd worn the night before. Maybe the toiletry bag, as well as the luggage, were FBI issue. Or maybe Jessie simply didn't bring personally revealing items with her on assignment, no matter how long it lasted. For some reason the idea pricked at him. And made him want to know more.

Jessie went to the bed and unzipped the duffel bag far enough to stuff the toiletry bag inside. She looked over her shoulder at him, a slender black brow arched. "The purchase records?"

He had gone over them. Repeatedly. But one of the problems of having multiple alpha males with purchasing power on any given ranch was that it created a jumble of receipts. Fortunately, he'd been able to sort through those of the Wright Ranch fairly quickly. Mostly because his family actually talked to each other. But Grant's were more troubling. At least since his daughter's fiancé had come on board.

Not willing to air his concerns just yet, he simply replied, "Working on it."

Her field-green gaze held his for a long moment as if trying to peer into his brain.

God help him if she actually could. Because damn, she was pretty. Still, he stared right back at her until she blinked and shifted her attention to rezipping her duffel.

Returning his hat to his head, Ian accepted that his attempt to snoop on the feds was a bust and went to take her suitcase so he could do as she'd asked and wheel it out to his truck.

Still typing away, Beck said, "Try to keep the pillow fights to a minimum, kids."

"Yes, Dad," Jessie returned in a perfect imitation of teenage exasperation.

Just as he'd thought earlier, no romantic vibes at all. Why the confirmation should send a rush of relief through him was beyond him.

Jessie slung her leather tote over one shoulder and started to pick up the clearly heavy duffel. He automatically took the straps from her and lifted the duffel from the bed. A metallic *thunk* sounded inside that she studiously ignored.

Somehow he doubted he'd just heard her curling iron hitting her hairdryer.

JESSIE WATCHED IAN hoist her suitcase into the bed of his dually pickup then take considerable care loading the duffel bag containing her firearms, as if he suspected what the duffel contained. His solemn dark blue gaze met hers across the truck bed and she smiled back at him, unrepentant. It wasn't as if she was here on vacation, after all.

Ian did not return her smile. But nor did he hustle around the truck to open her door for her, so maybe he was finally coming to understand that she could take care of herself.

They each climbed into their respective sides of the big truck and Jessie put her purse containing all her recording devices on the floorboard between her feet. Ian waited until she'd buckled her seat belt before starting the engine. Ever the caretaker.

A jab of longing behind her breastbone took her by surprise. Telling herself it was the glare of the morning sun making her vision swim, she ruthlessly squashed the stupid yearning, or whatever it was, and fished her sunglasses out of her purse. She didn't need some gorgeous cowboy worrying about her welfare. She could take care of herself.

Ian remained silent as he drove them through little Pineville toward the Wright Ranch. Was he regretting his very obvious attempt to get a look at what she and Peter were working on in their secure work space? He definitely didn't have a knack for that sort of thing. Because he was so honest? But if he was so squeaky clean, why hadn't he wanted her staying at the big house?

Because he wanted to keep an eye on her, that was why. Was he now also regretting his plan? Or was he plotting a new tactic? And why? If his family truly had nothing to hide as he'd repeatedly claimed, then why the curiosity?

Her suspicions stirring anew, Jessie plucked at her lower lip and watched Main Street Pineville go by. The worst part about this case was the sheer number of potential suspects.

"So many cowboys," she murmured.

"You say that like we're locusts."

She glanced at Ian, but his attention was still on the road. "Sorry."

"Why don't you like cowboys?" Ian asked with alarming perceptiveness.

Panic bubbled up Jessie's throat. No way could she tell

him her personal truth, so she punted by telling him the truth as it pertained to this assignment. "I was simply thinking about how many potential suspects there are here."

He looked at her, his deep blue eyes hard. "We're all cowboys, so we're all suspects?"

He'd pretty much hit the nail on the head, so she responded with a helpless shrug.

"Nice." He returned his attention to the road, heading them out of town toward his family's ranch.

Not wanting Ian to dwell on the fact that she considered everyone he knew and cared about a suspect in her investigation, she brought up the point she hoped would get her a room to stay in at the main house. "You realize your family will assume we're sleeping together."

A muscle in his jaw flexed. "I told them we're just friends."

She scoffed. "And they bought that like a three-legged race horse."

He shot her a quick glance, his eyebrows raised.

She shrugged again. "Would you be willing to take your *friend* to the rodeo Grant Williams mentioned last night?"

"I already planned on being there."

"To watch your brother compete in the bull riding?"

"Of course. Among other things."

Jessie waited for him to elaborate, but he fell silent again. She turned her attention back to the passing scenery, and when the arid land became lush, irrigated pastures and the fence lines changed from barbed wire to treated wood she knew they'd entered the realm of Thomas Wright.

The tall, scrolled iron gate was closed when they turned off the road, but Ian reached up and pressed a button above the windshield that would be a programmable garage door opener for plebeians like her. The gate instantly and smoothly swung open. Once they were through, it automatically closed behind them.

Ian drove them up the long, asphalt-paved driveway, but instead of entering the circular drive in front of the main house, he turned onto another driveway that led to a separate, oversized, six-bay garage. He steered the truck around the garage onto another paved drive that led to a separate single-story home that was at least three thousand square feet and built to mirror the big house. She had been expecting something quaint, at the very least utilitarian, when Thomas had mentioned the ranch manager's house. But Ian's home was as much of a showplace as the main house with its tile roof and stained cedar siding.

Her surprise must have read as questioning on her face because Ian made a sweeping gesture toward the house. "Welcome to the ranch manager's house."

"It's a beautiful home," she said truthfully.

"Thank you. I like it." He parked the truck in front of one of the two doors of the attached garage and climbed out.

Jessie grabbed her purse and followed suit. Before she could round the truck he'd already lifted her suitcase and duffel bag out of the back of the truck. She reached for the duffel to give him a hand.

"I've got it." He swung the straps over his shoulder and raised the pull handle on the suitcase. "Come on in." He hitched his head toward the front door in encouragement for her to follow him as he wheeled her suitcase onto the small gabled front porch.

Ian opened the front door and held it for her to proceed him into the house. She took two steps in and stopped, struck by the comfortable elegance of his home. The entryway opened directly to a great room with a stone fireplace reaching to the vaulted ceiling, overstuffed burgundy leather furniture, and slate flooring throughout. Opposite the fireplace was a large gourmet kitchen with tan-and-black-flecked granite slab counters and high-end stainless steel appliances. Across from the front door was a wall of windows showcasing the same incredible view of the snowcapped mountains shared by the back of the main house.

Ian's warm hand touched the small of her back, gently urging her forward and breaking the spell.

The heat of embarrassment flooded her. "I'm sorry." She stepped to the side so he could wheel her suitcase in. "Your home is just so . . . so . . . perfect." Totally the truth.

"Thanks," he said begrudgingly as he removed his cowboy hat and hung it on a rack full of hats next to the door. "The guest room is this way." Hitching her duffel bag's straps higher on his shoulder and pulling her suitcase behind him, he passed the kitchen and disappeared down a hall.

Jessie followed him, peeking through open doorways as she went. His office was in the first room she passed, and would be the first room she visited when the opportunity presented itself. The next open doorway revealed the guest room where Ian was removing an actual saddle from the footboard of the queen bed dominating the room.

"I'd assumed your grandfather was joking when he'd said you would need to clear your saddles out of the guest room."

"Saddle. Only one." He hoisted it in emphasis and looked around the room as if debating where to set it. He turned toward the small desk tucked against one wall, but it already boasted some sort of engine part atop a spread out newspaper. "I'd meant to clean all this out last night, but . . . I didn't," he explained, then seemed to make a decision. "Excuse me."

Jessie moved out of Ian's way, stepping back into the hall as he hauled the saddle out of the room and headed back down the hall, disappearing through a door that had been closed, presumably into the garage. Or maybe he had a tack room in the house. She'd put nothing past this family.

Knowing Peter would pitch a fit if she didn't check in, Jessie reached into her purse and retrieved her phone. She quickly texted *Here. All good.*

Peter immediately texted back *Roger that.*

Moments later Ian reappeared and strode back down the hall. He stepped by her to reenter the room, this time going to the desk and gathering the engine part up in the newspaper it sat upon. When he moved by her this time, he smiled sheepishly. "Seized transmission."

Jessie found herself smiling back at him and meaning it. How could such a big, commanding man be so cute?

He paused, as if her smile had momentarily derailed him. "I'll just put this . . . somewhere, too, and let you get settled." He used his elbow to gesture back at her suitcase which he'd parked next to the bed and the duffel he'd set atop the plush burgundy bedspread.

"Thank you."

He gave a small nod in acknowledgment and headed back down the hall.

She yanked her gaze away from his backside. *Cowboy cowboy cowboy*, she vigorously reminded herself.

Exactly, her libido shot back.

CHAPTER SEVEN

S EATED IN HIS office chair, Ian stared at the ATV transmission he'd dumped smack in the middle of his desk, trying to give his new houseguest the time to get settled as he'd promised. He'd intended to leave the transmission and the saddle in the guest room to hopefully shorten her stay. But when he'd seen her look of genuine admiration for his home, he couldn't bring himself to be inhospitable. His mom had raised him better.

He poked at the transmission. Luckily, he'd left the newspaper beneath the seized hunk of junk because it was oozing an oily fluid that would have ruined the fine wood grain beneath. Though it wasn't as if he'd left anything important out on the desk. He might be foolish, but he wasn't dumb. He'd filed away any ranch business papers and locked away his ledgers in the safe built into the cabinet behind him.

While his family had nothing to hide, he had no idea what a federal agent could use as probable cause, and he wasn't about to find out. As long as he was unable to control what she was looking for, he didn't want her looking. Period.

He had just started trying to read an article on a new

brewery opening in town through the leaked transmission fluid when a knock sounded on the door frame. He looked up to find Jessie standing expectantly in the doorway.

"Am I interrupting?" she asked.

He pushed back from the desk. "Not at all."

She gestured at the transmission. "Interesting paperwork you have there. Motorcycle transmission?"

"ATV."

She nodded sagely, her gaze sliding to his. "You're a fix-er, aren't you?"

"I've been known to be handy," he said, though he knew that wasn't what she meant. He took care of his family. He'd promised his mother he would. Even though he knew she hadn't been right in the head at the end, he'd still promised her. A promise he would always keep. He stood and rounded the desk. "Are you ready?"

"Sure." Her gaze darted back to the desk. She probably had hoped to find the Wright Ranch's entire financial history laid out for her inspection, not a useless ATV part. Her dark brows dipped and she looked back at him. "Ready for what?"

"To ride out to the south pasture and check out the steers grazing there as well as the view my grandfather told you about."

"I don't need—"

"My grandfather is expecting me to take you to look at the view. So I'm going to take you to look at the view. He'll know if I don't."

Her dark brows shot up. "Thomas Wright, the all-seeing?"

"Something like that." Ian had stopped trying to figure out how his grandfather always seemed to know what was happening around him a long time ago. Ian ran his gaze over her T-shirt and jeans, trying not to think about the curves beneath.

And failing.

He started to sweat. He forced his attention to her boots. "Good riding boots."

She looked down and shrugged. "They're comfortable."

He considered her glossy black hair and creamy complexion next. "Do you have a hat?"

"Yes. A baseball hat."

"That will work."

She grinned. "It says FBI."

"Ah. Never mind. I'm sure I can come up with something that will stay on your head and keep the sun off. Come on." He stepped past her and headed down the hall to get his own hat.

She didn't follow him immediately. She was probably staring longingly into his office, itching to pull open all those file cabinets. But then he heard the sound of her boot heels on the slate floor. Relief flooded him as he grabbed a knapsack off a kitchen bar chair and went into the fridge to load up on bottled water and snacks. Over his shoulder he asked, "Do you have a light jacket, or sweatshirt? One that doesn't say FBI? Just in case?"

"I do." She turned and hurried back to the guest room.

Pulling the cinch top of the knapsack closed, Ian snagged

his work cowboy hat from the hat rack.

Jessie reappeared with what looked to be a hooded windbreaker in her hand and followed behind him as he went to the sliding glass doors leading out back.

She said, "Is this really necessary? My time would be better spent going over any paperwork you'd be willing to share with me. Which should be all of it, if what you've been saying about your family's business dealings is true."

Namely, that they weren't crooks. He would have thought the help he'd provided their investigation thus far would have earned him some trust. Assuming Special Agent Jessie Martin was capable of trust. She very well might not be.

He opened the slider, taking a moment to pull in a deep breath of fresh air scented with grass and summer, then moved aside so she could go through first. "A lot of people work this ranch, and as ranch manager, they come looking for me if they have problems or needs. If one of the hands, or any of my family besides Liam, were to come through this door and find you poring over ranch paperwork, I'm pretty sure your cover would be blown."

Jessie stared out at his back deck, the crushed gravel path that led to the main house and stables, the lush lawn, the stained-wood fence line, pasture land, and mountains beyond.

She really didn't seem to like to give up the bit once she'd gotten it between her teeth. Too bad. Ian wasn't going to accommodate her. "If you still want me to take you to the rodeo this weekend so you can see for yourself what Grant is up to, you'd be smart to stick to your story."

Her green eyes narrowed.

Maybe bringing her intelligence into it wasn't the wisest thing to do. There was no question she was very, very smart. But it always worked with his sister and Amanda, so . . .

She huffed. "Fine. But let's not be gone all day."

"You did notice the size of this ranch, right?"

"Yeah, yeah." She waved off his reminder and stalked through the door.

Suppressing a grin, Ian put on his hat, stepped out into the warm morning, and closed the sliding glass door behind him. He liked her no-nonsense, almost brash way, which really set his teeth on edge. He shouldn't like her or admire the way she walked, or respect the fearlessness that fairly oozed off her.

She'd hesitated at the edge of his deck. When he reached her side she said, "Which way?"

It dawned on him she was confused. There was, after all, more than one stable, as well as the bull barn and the old barn. He pointed at the gabled stable nearest them. "That one. The saddle horse stable."

"Which makes that one . . . ?" She pointed at the larger stable.

"The bucking horse stable. Though I'm not sure for how much longer. Liam might take them with him over to Sky High Ranch after he marries Amanda."

Jessie squinted up at him. "Doesn't Amanda have a barrel racer program?"

"She does, thanks to you finding and returning her stolen stud to her. And it's why I say Liam might move his broncs next door."

She nodded and returned her gaze to the barns and out-buildings. "The bull barn is, well, obvious, but what's in that old barn?"

Did she ask so many questions because she was simply doing her job, or because she was inherently curious? Probably both. "Mostly equipment."

"Like all-terrain vehicles?" There was definite hope in her tone.

He pointed to the huge detached garage next to the house. "They're in the toy garage."

She laughed. "Of course they are. Any chance we could ride those out to the back pasture?"

"Nope." He stepped off the deck onto the path he took every morning to work.

She hurried to catch up with him. "Because one is currently lacking a transmission?"

He shortened his stride. "No. We have plenty. I know Grandfather, and he'll expect me to take you out on horseback to give you the full ranch experience. So that's what I'll do." Then he stopped in his tracks. "You can ride, right?"

She kept walking. "Don't worry. I'll figure it out."

Ian ran a hand over his face. He hadn't considered the fact that her entire cover story had been a lie. She'd sounded very convincing. But that was also part of her job, wasn't it? The fact she was such a convincing liar—a professional, actually—raised the hair on the back of his neck.

And was at complete odds with what the sway of her

backside as she continued on up the path was doing to the rest of him.

JESSIE FOCUSED ON the crunch of crushed gravel beneath her boots as she walked with Ian toward the stable. Not the bronc stable, mind you, but the saddle horse stable. Who had more than one horse stable? Very successful rodeo ranchers, that's who. She felt as if she'd been transported back into a childhood fantasy, back when she had still fantasized about something better. Not different, just better. She hadn't been too far into her teens when she realized only different would be better. But then she'd fallen in love, and had been willing to give up on her plans for a sweet-talking cowboy.

She was thankful Ian remained silent as they walked. The closer she and Ian drew to the beautiful stable, built and finished to mirror the homes on the property with stained cedar siding and a tiled and gabled roof, the greater her anxiety became. She had no idea how to play this. Did she pretend to be a complete novice on horseback? Or did she ride as if she'd been born into the saddle? Or somewhere in between? As she'd decided the night before at the engagement party, including some truth in a lie was always best, so in between it was. Which might not be difficult considering how long it had been since she'd been on a horse.

The big, double sliding stable doors stood open as they approached and she could hear a clear, masculine voice singing. When she realized what he was singing, her step faltered and she turned to look at Ian.

Amusement lightened the blue of his eyes. "That's Big Mike, one of the horse wranglers. He's a big Britney fan."

Jessie had no response to that, so she simply nodded and stepped inside.

And stopped in her tracks. She wasn't sure which she found more jaw-dropping, the sight of not so big Big Mike picking up an entire bale of hay as if it were a down pillow while singing, "Oops, I did it again," or the sheer beauty of the stable's interior. She decided the stable won out.

The open-beamed ceiling was clad with the same stained tongue and grove pine as Ian's house and the main house and matched the finish on the twelve stalls—six on each side of the wide center alley. Each stall was topped with elaborate wrought-iron scrollwork that was as functional as it was beautiful. Just like the big gate out front. And just like the rest of the ranch, the stable was spotless and meticulously maintained.

She pulled in a deep breath and smelled only commitment and pride.

The warm touch of Ian's hand on her back, urging her forward, jolted her out of her fanciful thoughts.

"Hey, Big Mike," Ian called out, moving past her into the stable.

The wrangler cut off his song and looked toward them. "Hey boss." His gaze landed on Jessie and his face lit up. "Special Agent Martin! So great to see you again." He set the hay bale down as if it weighed nothing and strode toward them.

Alarm shot through Jessie. She'd forgotten there had been a Wright Ranch hand over at Amanda's Sky High Ranch when Jessie had returned the stolen stallion. And it had indeed been Big Mike. She jerked her gaze to the rest of the stable behind Mike, assuring herself there was no one else within earshot. Other than the horses who'd stuck their heads over the tops of their stall doors at Big Mike's exclamation, they appeared to be alone.

Next to her, Ian muttered, "How the hell—?"

"He was watching over Amanda's place when we brought Whiskey Throttle back."

"Oh, yeah. I'd forgotten."

"So had I," she said darkly. In a different circumstance, forgetting a detail such as that could get her killed in her line of work. She'd let her guard down, which was unacceptable. She needed to be more careful.

Forcing herself to relax, Jessie accepted the wrangler's hand and shook it in greeting.

His voice low, Ian said, "Listen, Big Mike, Agent Martin is working undercover right now. We can't let anyone know she's FBI."

Big Mike's eyes rounded. "Oh, wow. Are you looking for the rustlers who have been hitting the ranches around here?"

She glanced quickly at Ian, who gave her a shrug that seemed to say *small town* by way of explanation.

Meeting Big Mike's excited gaze, she admitted, "I am." There wasn't much point in denying it when he already knew what she was.

"That's awesome. Those bastards need to be caught. So what do you want to be called?"

She smiled, ridiculously reassured by his response. "We're just going with Jessie Martin."

His sandy blond eyebrows twitched up. "Your real name?"

"Technically, my real name is Jessica Martin." She lifted one shoulder. There really wasn't the need to get into the slim odds of anyone feeling the need to research her identity.

"Ah, the old *keep it simple, stupid.* I like it." Big Mike grinned.

Ian said, "We're saying she's an old friend from college, pretty much just visiting."

Mike's eyebrows went up again. "Pretty much?"

"Pretty much." Ian nodded and handed her the black nylon knapsack before moving past Mike. "We're going to ride out to the back pasture and take a look at the rough stock steers. How is Chuck today?"

"Chuck is . . . Chuck." Big Mike looked her up and down. "How about Jilly?"

Ian made a noise as he dipped into what was probably the tack room. "Jilly gets bratty this time of year," he called from within.

"Right. Chuck it is."

The two men were obviously trying to match her to a suitable mount. But based on what, exactly? The urge to pick her own mount from the beautiful horses watching them from their stalls made Jessie itch.

She couldn't help herself from drifting over to the most

glorious palomino she'd ever seen. She offered her hand for what she assumed to be a gelding to smell and the big quarter horse arched his neck over the stall, rumbling deep in his throat when she smoothed her hand over his velvety muzzle and broad blond cheek.

Ian appeared on the other side of the horse's head. "I see you've met Clint."

"Clint?"

Big Mike emerged from a stall leading a beautiful black quarter horse with a white blaze down his face and two white socks on his hind legs. "Clint Eastwood. As in, *do you feel lucky, punk?*" He laughed.

Jessie frowned at the incongruency between the horse's clearly sweet nature and his movie tough-guy namesake.

"Ian is the only one who can ride him," Big Mike added, sliding a bridle onto Chuck's head.

Ian scrubbed behind Clint's ear. "He's a good boy. He just gets a little frisky sometimes."

Like the only man who can ride him?

Jessie blinked at the unexpected thought. Then she dismissed the notion outright. Ian Neisson was far too controlled to ever indulge in friskiness. Even if she wanted him to. Which she didn't. But there was no stopping the flush of heat rampaging through her body and flooding her face. She would not acknowledge just how much this man affected her. No way. No how.

"Here." Ian held a light brown felt cowboy hat up for her to take. "It's one of Caitlin's. She stashes hats everywhere because she always forgets to grab one before she leaves the house."

Jessie took the hat. It looked brand new. "Are you sure your sister won't mind?"

"Positive," Ian asserted as he clipped a lead on Clint's halter and lifted the latch on the stall door. "Pardon."

Jessie stepped out of the way so Ian could swing the door open and lead his horse out.

The minute Clint stepped from the stall Chuck let out the strangest noise as Big Mike saddled him.

Jessie looked to Ian in surprise.

He laughed. "Yep, Chuck is short for Chuckles. He has made that noise since he was a foal. Chuckling after his dam, his buddies, and anyone with a treat in their pocket."

Jessie was instantly enchanted. Quirky horses were the best.

It was a preference she'd buried deep. But now that it had resurfaced, it opened the door to a bone-deep longing for the freedom being on a horse had always given her.

No. Not now.

She was working. Working a job she adored. A job that would get her to a big city where there would be no place for quirky—let alone chuckling—horses.

Resisting the urge to offer her help, she settled her borrowed hat on her head and stood patiently, waiting for the men to saddle the horses. Ian attached saddle bags to the back of his saddle then took the knapsack and her jacket from her and tucked them inside.

Big Mike eyed her again, then changed the height of the stirrups. She could have told him which notch to thread the buckle through, but doing so would have outed her as a practiced horsewoman. So she remained silent until he was satisfied with his adjustments and called her over.

She tried to look as tentative and unsure as she could as she approached Chuck. She'd let Big Mike help her mount to further sell her inexperience. Though Ian was busy tightening the cinch on his saddle, she knew he was paying sharp attention to her. She could feel his gaze like it was . . . not a caress, but more like a claiming. She shook her head to dispel the ridiculous thought and focused on the horse in front of her.

The ranch hand smiled kindly at her. "That's right. He won't hurt you. Just come around to the left side to get on. Then take hold of saddle horn—"

"What about the reins?" Too much? Maybe.

"Don't worry about them. I'll hang on to them until you get settled. Grab the horn, get your left foot in the stirrup . . ."

Jessie did as he instructed. She grabbed hold of the saddle horn, giving it a slight tug to test the tightness of the cinch as subtly as she could, and lifted her boot toward the stirrup. Then what were beginning to be very familiar strong, warm hands gripped her waist and lifted her up. She couldn't help but squeak as she had to rush to swing her right leg over Chuck's back, plopping herself unceremoniously into the saddle.

She looked down at Ian, but he was busy settling her left boot into the stirrup and checking the depth of the bend in her knee. She'd always preferred her stirrups a little on the long side for more stability when cutting or sliding, but she kept her mouth tightly shut, her back teeth locked against the sensation of his hand feeling up her knee-pit.

Then he glanced up at her, his eyes sapphire blue in the natural light streaming in through the dormer windows. Her mind went blank.

"How does that length feel? Are you comfortable?"

Hell to the no. The way she felt looking down into his handsome face and, god help her, those eyes, was anything but comfortable.

She swallowed and nodded. "Yes. It's good."

"Good." Ian gave her leg a squeeze and a pat before turning to mount his horse.

A shiver of need coursed over her skin. The horse beneath her shifted his weight as if sensing her mood. Horses were sensitive that way.

You better not out me, buddy, she silently commanded.

Big Mike beamed at her. "You did great! Here, hold these in your left hand and just steer him in the direction you want him to go. But don't worry, he'll automatically follow Clint." He gave her the reins and moved off to the side and out of the way.

She smiled her thanks at the kind ranch hand as guilt for having to deceive him churned in her stomach. But she had to do what she had to do.

The moment Ian's backside hit the saddle, Clint began to dance. Ian easily controlled the muscular palomino with the reins and a shift of his weight. "Ready?" Ian asked.

"Ready," she said, automatically raising the reins to signal to the horse to move, which Chuck did.

Ian held Clint back to allow her and Chuck to precede him out of the stable. As soon as they were clear of the building and well into the knee-high late summer grass, Ian urged Clint to her side.

"How does it feel?" Ian asked her again.

"Great." She told him the truth. Being back in a saddle felt amazing. "It feels grea—" A flock of quail erupted from the grass, taking flight directly in front of Chuck, startling him into a sideways escape. Muscle memory took over and she leaned forward, brought her heels forward and gripped tight with her knees to keep her seat. She let Chuck move far enough away from where the birds had startled him for him to calm down before reining him back to Ian.

Holding his equally startled mount under control, Ian looked her straight in the eye and said, "You didn't grow up in some suburb in Colorado, did you?"

CHAPTER EIGHT

I AN'S HEART HAD leapt into his throat when the covey of quail erupted in flight right under the horses' noses, sending Chuck into a sideways bolt. While Clint danced beneath him, Ian had watched in horror as the black quarter horse gelding tried to escape what had frightened him as quickly as he could.

Usually, when a horse crow-hopped or just plain skittered sideways in fear, their rider was left straddling air. But Jessie had stuck like a tick to the horse's back, using her legs and even her hands on the reins to maintain her center of balance in the saddle and gain control of the panicked horse.

An experienced rider move if he'd ever seen one.

Clearly, the story she'd told his dad and grandfather about growing up in a suburb of Denver hadn't been true. So he'd called her on it.

"What?" she said, trying to work the still spooked gelding back toward him. She allowed Chuck to keep his head low so he could scan the suddenly very scary grass in front of him as he quivered and blew great huffs of air.

"I said, you did not grow up in some suburb, did you? You grew up on a ranch in Colorado, didn't you?"

"No, I did not."

He guided Clint toward her and Chuck. "Don't lie to me, Jessie. You clearly know how to ride. And ride well. That was totally a cutting horse rider move." Had anything she'd told him been true?

"I'm not lying, Ian. I didn't grow up on a ranch in Colorado." She heaved a sigh and ran a soothing hand over Chuck's neck. "It was in Nevada. I grew up on a cattle ranch in Nevada. Which is why my bosses tapped me for this assignment."

"Why not just say so?"

She rolled her eyes. "It's called undercover for a reason."

Her excuse didn't ring true. He narrowed his eyes at her.

Jessie met his gaze briefly, then resumed soothing Chuck. "We should keep going. So he won't become afraid of this field."

Ian looked around to see if anyone else had witnessed her feat of horsemanship. No one appeared to be in sight. Not surprising with a rodeo coming up this weekend. "And to keep up your pretense."

"You mean my cover?"

"Yes, your cover." Cover, pretense . . . whatever name she wanted to use, it was still lies. He'd known who and what she was, so he didn't know why the fact that she'd created an entire persona from scratch, had kept very basic truths about herself hidden from him, bothered him so much.

He watched her stroking Chuck's gleaming neck, her long braid, just as black and shiny, sliding over her shoulder.

He pulled his gaze away, focusing on the irrigated grass dancing in the gentle breeze. Maybe her deception bothered him so much because he wouldn't know what to believe and what not to believe.

As if sensing she was about to lose his cooperation, her tone turned conciliatory, "Look, why don't we go for a ride? Though, it would be best if we didn't go too far. It's been a very long time since I've been in a saddle, and I can already tell I'll pay for it tomorrow." She smiled.

He realized with a jolt he could tell the difference between her genuine smile, which she'd just sent him, and her *cover* smile. Her green eyes shone like grass lit by the summer sun when her smile was real.

And it left his mouth dry and his palms damp.

Lucky for him she didn't seem too inclined to really smile very often.

The horses had calmed. The quail, with their short bursts of flight, were whistling and clicking in the tall grass about twenty yards to their left. So Ian reined Clint to the right.

As he went by her he said, "Fine. But we still need to ride to the south pasture."

"Why? Trust me when I say I have zero need to check out some view."

Trust her? He snorted. That option had gone out the window when she'd had him called in to the sheriff's station and placed in an interrogation room to be given the Men in Black treatment by her and her partner.

Over his shoulder he said, "Because my grandfather expects us to. He'll want to know how the steers pastured there looked." Ian faced forward. "I've lied to him enough already. I'm not going to lie to him about this."

"Fair enough."

Keeping an eye out for any other surprises in the tall, late summer grass, Ian led the way through the series of gates that allowed access to all the individual pastures, deftly opening and closing them without having to dismount. Definitely one of the perks of traveling on horseback instead of riding an ATV. Plus there was no risk of igniting the dry grass into a fire with the hot undercarriage of the four wheelers—that would definitely ruin everyone's day.

They rode in silence, companionably, he might have said, under different circumstances. But that emerald gaze of hers saw everything—the yearling bulls yet to start their training, the breeding heifers and their calves, Liam's bucking broncs—and even though there was nothing to hold against his family for her to see, he couldn't relax.

They crested a small rise dominated by a stand of tightly bunched aspens and came upon the herd of steers the Wright Ranch contracted out to rodeos in the region for steer roping and wrestling congregated in a slight depression below. Ian guided them into the trees' dappled shade.

"They look good."

He studied her profile. Her face was shadowed by her hat and hidden from the filtered sun. "Did your family raise stock for rodeos?"

She shook her head, but didn't look at him. Nor did she clarify.

"Did you, or your family, rodeo?"

Again with the silent head shake.

Okay. Clearly she preferred to ask the questions, not answer them. Very irritating. "Tomorrow we'll cut out a dozen or so, drive them in, load 'em up, and take them to the county rodeo grounds."

"Can I come?"

And they were back to her agenda. Extremely irritating. "I'll take you when the rodeo actually starts. Grant won't be there until then."

She made a face and shifted in the saddle, clearly not liking his answer. Then she turned toward him, lifted her chin, and met his gaze. "Will you help me navigate behind the scenes? Get me in where they don't normally let just anyone?"

All his brain could register was how pretty she was. Her green eyes, heart-shaped face, silky long black hair, and sleek figure completely derailed him. It spoke to a part of him he'd denied for so long, the part that would have lived for himself instead of keeping true to the promise he'd made.

"Will you?" she pressed when he didn't answer.

He forced himself to look away. "I said I would."

"And you always do what you say you're going to do?" She didn't bother to hide her skepticism.

"I do." She could doubt all she wanted. He was a man of his word.

"Good to know." She didn't sound convinced.

He didn't care.

Her attention slid to his saddlebag. "So what, exactly, did you pack in that knapsack of yours?"

"Hungry?"

"I'd forgotten how much of an appetite riding could give you."

"Didn't have your cowboy breakfast this morning?"

"I did not. I'm not much of a breakfast person. I did, however, mean to eat a protein bar, but my transportation showed up way early." A genuine smile.

He dismounted and ground tied Clint to keep himself from staring. "Sorry about that."

"You can make it up to me by feeding me now." She dismounted with practiced ease and dropped the reins as he had, correctly assuming Chuck was trained not to go anywhere with his reins on the ground as Clint was.

How could he have ever thought her inexperienced?

He pulled the nylon knapsack from his saddlebag and carried it to the thick base of a double aspen where he took a seat.

She reached down into her boot and pulled her phone out.

Did the other boot contain her firearm?

She saw him watching her and raised the cell phone. "I need to check in with Peter," she explained and stepped back into the sunshine, away from the horses, without waiting for his reply.

And what could he have said? He was very aware she was working. He watched her long black hair dance in the slight breeze for a moment then lifted his gaze to the expanse of blue sky visible between the Aspen leaves. There was just enough breeze to make them dance with the noisy rattle they were famous for. He needed to keep the fact that she was an FBI agent working a case in the forefront of his mind. This was not some quasi date picnic. Not in any reality.

He dropped his gaze to where she had wandered. She appeared to be texting, but he could swear she also took a picture of the herd of steers.

It set Ian's teeth on edge.

After slipping her phone back into her boot, Jessie returned to his spot under the trees and plopped next to him with surprising disregard for the backside of her jeans. "Nice spot."

"It is." He opened the drawstring top of the bag and fished out a bottle of water. He gave it to her. "I often come here and just sit. I used to think I was the only one until I finally noticed this . . ." He tapped the trunk of the tree she'd leaned against.

She twisted to see what he was talking about, then barked out a laugh. "Ian eats Buckaroo Banzai shit," she read aloud what had been carved into the soft bark of the aspen, tracing the deep groves with her finger. She raised a dark brow at him. "Wow. Carving that took some effort. Dare I ask?"

"Buckaroo Banzai is the name we—my siblings and I—gave the practice bucking barrel I'd strung between two trees near the house when we were kids." He pulled the apples and granola bars from the bag, giving Jessie one of each. "Apparently one of them—still don't know who—thought I hit the dirt beneath the barrel a little too often."

"Did you?"

"Absolutely. Have you ever tried staying on one of those things while your rowdy siblings tried to bounce you off?"

"I have not."

There was something about the way she said it, a faint sadness, that made him ask, "Do you have any brothers or sisters?"

She plucked the short stem from the apple and flicked it into the grass. "No. I'm an only child."

Ian couldn't imagine life on a working ranch of any sort without a pack of kids to entertain each other. Had the solitude set her on her present course? "What made you want to be an FBI agent?"

"Them asking me to be. It had never entered my mind until I was recruited." She smiled at him, but it didn't reach her eyes. "Did you want to be a bull or bronc rider when you were younger?" She deftly changed the subject.

He decided to let it slide. For now. "Bull rider for a hot second. But then, as my sister puts it, I grew a brain."

Jessie's gaze searched his face for a long moment. A highly developed BS detector had probably been a job requirement. Besides, she had to know his family's history.

Thankfully she didn't comment on it, instead saying, "Well, if my opinion is worth anything, I think you made the right choice."

"Thank you." He relaxed back against the tree and took a long draw from his water bottle.

Considering the fact she was a federal agent snooping into his family and friends' dealings, her opinion was worth a whole hell of a lot. Their future was in her hands.

JESSIE GRIT HER teeth against the pain in her legs and backside as she walked with Ian back to the ranch manager's house from the saddle horse stable. Obviously she didn't have to wait until tomorrow to feel the burn of long-unused muscles.

After they had eaten everything Ian had brought with them in the knapsack, Ian had taken her on a tour of what seemed was the entire ranch, but she knew from her research on the ranch that he'd only shown her a sliver of the huge property despite the fact they had been in the saddle for the better part of the day.

"How long has it been since you've been in the saddle?" Ian asked.

Damn it. She'd hoped the brim of her borrowed cowboy hat would hide her grimace. Ian hadn't allowed her to return Caitlin's hat to the tack room, insisting she'd want something that didn't have FBI emblazoned on it to protect her from the sun when they attended the rodeo. He was right, so she'd kept the hat on.

She couldn't quickly think of any reason not to tell him the truth. "Ten years." Since she left home the day she turned eighteen.

"Well there you go. You'd be sore even without having to fight for your seat like you did when Chuck decided to go perpendicular on you."

His very accurate description of the spooked horse made her laugh. "He did make me work for it, that's for sure. But you can't blame him. Those birds bursting up out of the grass right under our noses scared the crap out of me too."

Jessie considered it sheer luck that she hadn't ended up flat on her back in the grass staring up at the sky, which would have hurt a lot more than simply being sore.

But man, was she sore. "I thought I was in good enough shape to avoid the worst of this." She groaned aloud when she ascended the two shallow steps to Ian's back deck. "I was wrong. So wrong."

Ian chuckled, a deep, rich sound that did funny things to her insides. "That's why I have that." He pointed to a hot tub built into the corner of the deck.

She hadn't noticed it previously because it was on the other side of two oversized, padded rocking chairs and foot rests with a glass-topped drink table set between.

"Did you pack a swimsuit?"

"Seriously?" Of course she hadn't packed a swimsuit. And not just because the Pineville Motel didn't have a pool. She was on assignment, working twenty-four-seven.

"I'll take that as a no. And it's not a problem. I have plenty of T-shirts and shorts you can wear into the hot tub."

The thought of wearing something of Ian's, wet and plastered against her skin, made Jessie's cheeks flush with heat. Good lord, now he had her blushing. She couldn't remember the last time she'd blushed.

It was when a cowboy whispered in my ear how badly he wanted to see my hair spread out on his pillow for the rest of his life, that's when.

She straightened her spine and folded her hands in front

of her. "You know, I'm sure a hot shower will work just as well as the hot tub."

Ian slid open the glass door. "Nonsense. If you don't soak those muscles you're not going to be able to walk tomorrow." He eyed her for a moment before stepping aside to allow her to go first into the house. "You can have the tub to yourself."

"No, that's not it. I don't need the tub to myself. I just—" She was just making a fool of herself. And she could certainly find something of her own that was suitable to wear. "You're right." She walked past him into the coolness of his beautiful house. "I do need to soak or I won't be able to get out of bed tomorrow, and I'd appreciate the company." She wasn't on vacation, after all. She was here to learn more about what these people did and how and if there was indeed a mysterious flash drive or other record as Karl Fletcher claimed.

Behind her she heard him trip on the sill.

She glanced back to make sure he was okay, but he was closing the sliding glass door, his face hidden by the brim of his hat.

He turned without looking at her and said, "I'll get you something to wear."

"That's okay. I can wear my workout clothes."

"Are you sure? Because I can loan you something, no problem."

"I'm sure. The odds of me getting up early tomorrow and going for a run are one hundred percent zilch."

His gaze traveled over her in a way that raised her temperature. "I think you can afford to miss a day or two."

Her waistline might be able to afford missing a workout, but her sanity? Jessie wasn't so sure.

"I'll change, grab towels, and meet you back out here in a few," Ian said.

"Okay." Jessie went to the guest room and changed as quickly as her rapidly tightening muscles would allow, mentally going over the questions she would ask Ian. Nothing like a relaxing soak in a hot tub to loosen the tongue as well as the muscles.

Donned in her jogging bra, white tank top, and black nylon running shorts and with her hat smashed hair up in a messy bun, she returned to the great room. The slate floor was cold on her bare feet.

Ian was standing in the kitchen pouring two glasses of what looked to be lemonade and wearing nothing but red, black, and white board shorts, a beach towel draped over one shoulder. Another towel lay folded on the counter next to the clear plastic glasses he was filling.

Jessie had known Ian was big, fit, and trim. He was tall with broad shoulders and a trim waist. But seeing his defined muscles on glorious display brought her up short.

He glanced up at her, his dark blue eyes bright, his hair tousled as if he'd run both hands through it, probably after removing his hat. His gaze flitted over her tank top and shorts. "Must have been fun figuring out how to hide a wire under that."

His stark reminder of what she was doing here nearly sent her back a step. But she held her ground despite the unexpected hurt flaring in her chest. "I'm officially clocked out."

"For some reason I doubt that very much. Lemonade?"

She studiously ignored the very accurate jab. "Yes, please." He could have offered her a glass of mud and she would have thanked him for it. The man was stupid gorgeous. "Can I help you with anything?"

"If you can grab this other towel and open the glass door, that would be great." He returned the lemonade pitcher to the fridge.

"Got it." She snagged the towel he'd brought out for her and went to slide open the glass door.

When Ian walked past her, she could smell his heat, his allure. She had to fight the urge to step back. To protect herself.

She waited a beat after he'd gone outside to follow him, pulling the glass door closed behind her. The late afternoon was still warm, but the crisp breeze was picking up and hinted at the fall just around the corner.

Ian had set the filled glasses atop the small table between the rocking chairs and dropped his towel onto a footrest so he could lift the brown fitted cover from the tub.

"Do you need any help?" she asked, her gaze drawn to sculpted muscles on his back, moving and flexing beneath his skin. There was nothing on this earth like true cowboy muscles. Nothing at all.

"No, I got it." He lifted the clearly heavy hot tub cover as if it weighed nothing. "But could you grab the lemonade?"

"Of course." She set her towel on top of his and picked up the glasses, bringing them over to the tub.

Ian eased himself into the tub, sighing as he submerged himself, then hit the jets on the tub's control panel. "It's a little hot, but running the jets will cool it some."

"I'm good with hot," she said as she handed him his glass of lemonade.

His gaze collided with hers and froze her with its intensity. Why was it that everything she said to this man came across like a come-on?

Maybe because her subconscious thought it was way past time for her to have a little adult fun.

Way past.

And Ian Neisson was the first man she'd met in a very, very long time to stir that part of her.

Great. Just great.

She jerked her gaze away from his and purposefully, carefully, set her drink into one of the tub's molded drink holders and stepped into the tub. Ian's strong hand closed around her biceps, ostensibly to steady her. Normally she would have thrown off the touch of a man who tried to get handsy with her. But she allowed Ian his chivalry. She would have blamed sunstroke, but she'd been wearing a very nice, very adequate hat and it hadn't been that hot.

She was definitely hot now. But at least she could blame the bubbling water she'd submerged herself into up to her chin.

"Thanks," she said, easing back into the molded seat that offered her the most panoramic view of the central Cascade Mountain range she'd ever seen.

"No problem. Better?"

"Yes. Oh my god, yes. You were right."

"It happens occasionally."

"I'm sure more often than that." From what she'd heard, the people in the area's rodeo community, as well as his family, thought very highly of Ian Neisson. Something that didn't happen unless he was right more than occasionally.

He lifted a bare, sculpted shoulder out of the water in a self-deprecating shrug.

Something else she liked. The man was humble.

Gorgeous, capable, and humble. Literally her perfect man. Except for the fact he was part of her current investigation.

And a cowboy.

"Do you miss it?"

She had to blink to focus. "Miss what?"

"Being on a ranch. Riding."

The truth hit her like a dually truck at highway speeds. She briefly touched the tiny gold horseshoe charm resting in the hollow of her throat from its delicate chain before returning her hand to beneath the water. "I do, actually."

"Why did you leave?"

She knew he meant the ranch she'd grown up on. "Well, for starters, it wasn't this." She made an expansive, dripping gesture toward the bright green, irrigated pasture land, the pristine fence line, the jaw-dropping main house, and the snowcapped mountains in the distance.

She could feel his gaze on her. He was smart enough to know that someone didn't leave the ranching life simply because they didn't live on a legacy ranch. She sighed and admitted, "I didn't have a place there. My stepfather didn't really take to me, and my mom . . . well, she was very taken with my stepfather."

"And your dad?"

"Didn't know him." She had never admitted as much to anyone as an adult. The one person she had told as a teen had crapped all over the intimacy.

"I'm sorry." He sounded sincere. She kept her gaze on the distant mountains instead of looking into his eyes to make sure. "So you left the ranch for the big city and never looked back."

"Pretty much."

"Except for that." He pointed at the base of her throat and it took her a moment to realize he was talking about her gold horseshoe necklace.

She reflexively reached up and touched it again.

"I've noticed you never take it off. Was it a gift?"

"To myself. I bought it when I left for college. A reminder, of sorts, that I can make my own luck."

"I'd assumed as much when we first met, but the more I get to know you, the more I think you're not the sort of person who needs to rely on luck." He smiled knowingly.

Her mouth went dry. "What sort of person, exactly, do you think I am?"

"The sort with enough brains and skill to get the job done."

His praise had her shifting uncomfortably on the molded seat.

"As well as the sort to never stop loving horses."

"You at least have that right," she admitted with a shrug. Then, having cracked open the truth door, she added, "I really miss riding."

"I'm glad I could give you today."

She met his dark blue gaze, and something shifted in her chest. "So am I."

CHAPTER NINE

IAN DIDN'T SLEEP for shit that night.

As he'd tossed and turned, he'd told himself it was because he was listening for any sound of Special Agent Jessica Martin leaving her room to go poking around in his office. But he knew, unequivocally, that he was full of crap.

He hadn't been able to fall into the sleep his exhausted body so desperately needed because the image of Jessie Martin rising from the hot tub with her tank top and running shorts plastered to her stunning body, the delicate horseshoe necklace glinting in the hollow of her throat, had been burned into his brain. There forever to torture him with what he could not—dare not—have.

It wasn't as if her wet clothing had been risqué, because it hadn't been. She'd worn a sports bra under her tank and her running shorts had been perfectly modest. But with her black hair and green eyes, she had an almost feline sensuality and grace that shut his brain off. At least, the one in his head. The southern one seemed to be working just fine.

Of all the women in the world to do this to him, why her? Her literal mission was to find fault with the people he had vowed to protect. He knew his mom wasn't all there when she'd elicited the vow, but he'd made it anyway. And it was a vow he intended to keep.

So he'd stayed awake, listening for the sound of an opening door that never came.

Seated at the kitchen bar, Ian was on his third cup of coffee, trying to clear the fog and the image of glistening skin from his mind, when he finally heard the guest room door open. He stilled, listening as her boot heels rapped their way down the hall.

When she reached the kitchen and saw him, she smiled. Her real smile. It hit him like a hoof to the chest.

Today she'd dressed in a pair of faded jeans, a lightweight, long-sleeve button-down shirt with narrow blue and white stripes, and her worn cowboy boots. The word *gorgeous* didn't do her justice. *Perfect*, maybe.

Despite the coffee he'd drank, his throat turned suddenly dry, but he managed to say, "Good morning."

"Morning." She raised her nose into the air, closed her eyes, and pulled in a deep breath. "Mmm, cowboy coffee. Smells wonderful."

Her obvious pleasure had his skin tightening. "Let me pour you a cup?" He started to rise from his stool but she held up a staying hand.

"I can get it." She went to the coffee maker and picked up the white porcelain mug he'd set out for her.

To keep from staring at her shapely backside, he buried his nose in his own mug. He seriously needed to get a grip. "Sleep well?"

"I did, actually." She sounded surprised.

"Nothing like a day of sun and saddle to give you a good night's rest." Unless there was the image of a sexy federal agent tormenting you.

She glanced over her shoulder. "Don't forget the hot tub."

He should live so long. The image of her rising out of the steaming water would be with him for a very long time. "And soaking in a hot tub," he agreed. "How do your muscles feel?"

She returned the coffee carafe to its heating plate. "Better than I expected, actually. I'm still a little sore, but it's not too bad."

"Good. And walking around the rodeo grounds will help as well."

She took a sip of coffee, her green eyes sharp on him over the rim of the mug. "You're still game to take me?"

"I said I would."

"Excellent. Just confirming." She carried her coffee to the counter across from him. "Do we have time for me to buy you breakfast at that little diner on Main Street? It's the least I can do to repay you for grilling that wonderful steak for me last night."

"That's not necessary." Fresh, quality steak was a perk of running a cattle ranch. And busying himself at the grill was the only way he could think of to stop himself from staring at her even after she donned sweatpants and an oversized hooded sweatshirt. "But yes, we do."

"Perfect." She downed her cup of strong, black coffee like a true cowhand—or a dedicated member of law enforcement. He had to remember that was exactly what she was. At all times.

THE COUNTY RODEO grounds weren't all that different from the rodeo and fairgrounds near Jessie's hometown in Nevada. Which wasn't near at all to her family's remote ranch. But they'd occasionally made the trek anyway, just for something to do. Same dust, same smells, same current of excitement and expectation.

The view here was decidedly better, though, even discounting Ian Neisson. The mountains appeared impossibly close and the sky incredibly blue. It really was pretty here.

Jessie hung back as Ian shook hands with yet another cowboy. Or maybe a stock contractor. It was hard to tell the difference with everyone pitching in with the unloading of the animals from the trailers into their pens.

Ian would inquire about the man's health, the wellbeing of his family and stock, and the prospects of the day. She pretended not to be listening—as she did just that—feigning interest in whatever animals were contained by whatever pen they happened to be standing near. Or the arena. Or the grandstands, where Peter was keeping vigil. They'd decided to forgo her wearing any recording or communication devices because with the general noise of the rodeo, the crowd, and PA system, the devices wouldn't be very effective.

But she mostly kept an eye out for Grant Williams. Short of finding the supposed record of the livestock thefts outright, discovering exactly what type of business Grant intended to do here at the rodeo was their current goal. Peter was in the grandstands on the off chance Grant hadn't been joking when he'd said he would do his business there. And as Ian helped her navigate behind the scenes, she watched for Grant.

At least she did when Ian wasn't distracting her. She couldn't help but be impressed by how many people knew and clearly respected him, and not simply because he was Thomas Wright's grandson. He appeared to know a little about every single person they encountered and always had a kind word, encouragement, or timely bit of advice.

Keeping track of who, what, where, and when was a necessary skill for her job. Ian seemed to do it, and do it effortlessly, because he genuinely cared about the members of the area's rodeo community.

"Is this the pretty lawyer friend of yours we've been hearing so much about?" the older gentleman Ian was currently talking to asked.

Ian reached to snag her elbow and drew her closer, his smile tight. "Jacob, I'd like you to meet Jessie Martin. Jessie, this is Jacob Hadley of the Hadley Cattle Company. Bodie, Garrett, and Ben's father."

Jacob was a direct competitor with the Wright Ranch for rodeo rough stock contracts as well as Ian's sister Caitlin's soon to be father-in-law. And, if his other two sons were to be believed, a recent victim of the rustlers.

She smiled brightly and shook his hand. "It's a pleasure to meet you, Mr. Hadley."

"Please, call me Jacob." He beamed at her and sent Ian an approving nod.

"I had the chance to meet your sons, Garrett and Ben, at the livestock auction. They mentioned something about you having some cattle stolen recently. Please tell me you were able to recover them."

Jacob waved off her concern. "I'm sure they'll turn up."

Ian gave her elbow a subtle squeeze before releasing her.

She received the hint that Jacob was the type of rancher who didn't want to be known for not being able to keep track of his money on the hoof. She let the matter drop. She could always track Garrett or Ben down to learn the particulars of the theft.

A hand clapped down on Ian's shoulder. "Ian, my boy. Showing off this pretty gal of yours, I see," Grant Williams chortled.

"How're you doing today, Grant?" Ian asked, deftly ignoring Grant's comment about her being his pretty gal.

"I'm doing very well, thank you."

Jacob exclaimed, "Grant! Just the man I was looking for."

Ian's gaze collided with hers briefly. Yep, welcome to the club.

"Here I am. I had my boys cut those cows we were talking about, so you can drop by anytime and take a look at them."

Jacob said, "I do appreciate that, but it can wait. I'm sure you're swamped with all the wedding rigmarole."

"Trust me, at this point, I can put on a wedding for that

girl in my sleep."

Jacob subtly held up three fingers and waggled them along with his eyebrows.

Grant heaved a sigh. "Hopefully this one will stick." He looked at Jessie and Ian. "You two need to come. If I'm going to throw yet another wedding for that daughter of mine, I'm going to invite people I actually like."

Ian said, "Jessie won't—"

"I'd love to," she cut him off. "Thank you so much for the invitation."

"My pleasure. And can I just say how happy I am to see this boy finally tending to his own needs, so to speak." Grant practically guffawed and slapped Ian on the back.

"So to speak," Jacob repeated on a chuckle.

Ian smiled patiently but didn't comment.

Grant said, "Say, do you know when that little brother of yours is slated to ride?"

"I don't, sir, other than that he's in pool B. But I can find out the exact time."

"No need. I was going to head up to the announcer's booth presently to make sure Pat gives my bulls their due. I can check the official schedule then." Grant turned to her. "If I don't see you again before, I'll look forward to seeing you out at my place this weekend."

"I will too. Thank you again for the invite."

"You are very welcome." Grant leaned toward Ian. "She sure is pretty. Don't let her get away."

Ian tipped his hat to his grandfather's friend, then threaded his arm around hers to draw her away.

As soon as they were out of earshot, Ian asked, "Will that do?"

She grinned up at him. "That'll do."

"Do you need to stay?"

"Are you trying to get rid of me, Mr. Neisson?"

"Not at all. But you wanted to find Grant, which we did. I have to check to see if Liam needs any help with his broncs and then check on the roping and wrestling steers. You're more than welcome to come with me, but I hate to waste your time, and I'll gladly take you wherever you'd like to go."

"Like back to your house?"

He opened his mouth, then snapped it shut. She could practically see him imagining her rifling through his desk and file cabinets, maybe even fixing his ATV transmission.

She reached with her free hand to pat his biceps, which flexed at her touch, and took pity on him. "I was thinking of that wonderful hot tub of yours, Ian."

Worry instantly clouded his blue eyes. "Are you okay? Are your muscles tightening up again?"

His concern stopped her in her tracks. Then she realized he was just being Ian. Always the big brother, always the caretaker. Hadn't she been watching examples of it all day? "No. I'm fine. I swear."

His gaze searched her face, then he nodded.

"Peter is in the grandstands. I'll go and find him, and we'll watch the rodeo while you work." And while they worked.

"Okay. Call me if you need anything."

"Same."

His face cleared and he smiled, his eyes crinkling at the corners. "Right. See you in a bit." He patted her hand, which she belatedly realized was still on his arm, before releasing her and striding away.

Her phone pinged with an incoming message, making her jump. She retrieved it from her back pocket and read the text.

Are you watching his butt as he walks away?

Good lord, she had been.

Though she had no idea exactly where Peter was, he clearly could see her. She turned toward the grandstands that were on the other side of the arena from where she stood and glared.

Then she texted him back. *Where are you?*

Center grandstand, seven rows up.

She focused on the middle of the covered grandstand, counting seven bench rows up until she spotted her fellow agent watching her through a small pair of binoculars. Not the most inconspicuous form of surveillance, but thankfully rodeo was a sport, after all. Some fans needed the up-close and personal experience.

He raised a hand in acknowledgment.

Jessie made her way around the white painted metal bull and bronc pens, funnel chutes, and the entrance and exit ally for the arena. The gate leading from the competitors' side of the arena and the spectators was manned by security, and she belatedly realized she might not be allowed back through. Fortunately the guard had no problem with her going into the stands.

She climbed the stands and sat down next to Peter, who'd set the binoculars down and picked up a bag of popcorn.

He tilted the bag toward her. "Popcorn?"

"Thanks." She took a handful.

"Nice hat. It suits you."

"It's Caitlin Neisson's," she said around a handful of very salty popcorn. Her favorite. "Her brother let me borrow it."

"Loaning out his sister's stuff to you . . ." Peter nodded slowly. "You know he watches your butt when you walk away too?"

"He does not."

Peter grabbed the binoculars and raised them. "Surveillance says otherwise."

Jessie shoved another handful of popcorn in her mouth. Normally, she'd be pleased to hear her attributes were working in her favor. But after seeing Ian wearing nothing but swim trunks . . . knowing he was looking back at her simply made her sweat. She found him far too attractive for her sanity's sake.

Peter asked softly, "Was that Grant you were talking to?"

"It was. As well as Jacob Hadley. Apparently Mr. Williams has offered to sell some cows to Mr. Hadley to replace the ones that were stolen."

"Jacob Hadley was not on our list of reported victims. I double-checked after his sons mentioned it at the auction."

"That's because it appears he didn't report it. When I told him Garrett and Ben had mentioned it, he said, and I quote, 'I'm sure they'll turn up.'"

"But why? Why not report the theft of thousands of dollars' worth of assets?"

"Pride, I suppose."

Peter shook his head. "Well, I think it's strange. Keeping silent makes it easier for the bad guys to do their thing. Ooh! Shaved ice." Peter waved over the vendor working the stands. "I had no idea rodeos were like ball games."

"It is a spectator sport, you know."

Peter paid for his cone of ice and rainbow-colored syrup and thanked the vendor, who continued his way up the grandstands. "Huh. Who knew."

Jessie laughed. "Actually, an awful lot of people. Remind me how you were assigned to this case again?"

"I'm an expert in interstate commerce and finance. And black-market trade, of course."

"Of course." With Peter distracted by the shaved ice, which was already turning his lips an odd brown color, Jessie went to work on the popcorn. "Oh, and Grant invited me to his daughter's wedding this weekend at his ranch."

Peter sputtered. "What? Why didn't you lead with that?"

She shrugged.

"Isn't that a big deal?"

"I got the impression his daughter had been married more than once before."

"Is that when he'll do his deal with Jacob Hadley?"

"Probably before, but they weren't specific. Mr. Williams simply told Mr. Hadley that he'd had his men cut the cows they'd talked about from the herd and invited Mr. Hadley to come by anytime and take a look at them."

"Sounds like they were referring to specific cows. Any idea why?"

"Not really. Other than the fact the cows stolen from the Hadleys were part of their bucking bull breeding program."

"Hmm. What do you think the odds are of you being able to check the brands or tags of those cows while you're there for the wedding?"

She gave him a look. "These ranches are big, Peter."

"But don't you think Mr. Williams would make it easy for Mr. Hadley to see them?"

She shrugged. "I guess there is only one way to find out."

Peter nodded in agreement. "I'd say this has been a good day, all and all." He saluted her with his cone then slurped as much of the syrup as he could. "But now what?"

She stretched her legs out and crossed her ankles. "Now we watch the rodeo."

Jessie had to explain most of the events to Peter, but when evening approached and the marque event of bull riding started, she found herself focused more on watching for Alec Neisson and, more specifically, his oldest brother, than answering Peter's questions.

It wasn't far into the event when Alec's name came up on the electronic reader board, and the announcer proclaimed an epic matchup was to be had with the relative newcomer attempting to ride Red Rum.

Peter mused ominously, "Red Rum? That does not sound good."

But Jessie's gaze was glued to the raised platform above

the chute where several men were preparing the bull and helping a lanky rider who she recognized as Alec despite the bulky protective vest and helmet with its wire face guard. And there was no doubt the broad-shouldered cowboy leaning over the chute and holding the front of Alec's vest, ready to yank him out of harm's way if the bull tried to stack him up in the chute, was Ian.

Jessie was mesmerized. She half expected Ian to refuse to relinquish his hold on his baby brother. Knowing Alec was so blatantly putting himself in danger must be excruciating for Ian. Everyone who knew him spoke of his dedication to protecting his family. Jessie couldn't even imagine having someone like him in her life.

But the moment Alec nodded and the gate was pulled open, Ian released Alec.

The huge bull, that was indeed red, bucked and spun as if he intended murder. And in less than two seconds sent Alec flying like a lawn dart into the deep dirt of the arena. But rather than going after Alec, Red Rum trotted to the exit alley, his workday done.

Alec scrambled to his feet and brushed himself off, seeming unharmed by the experience.

Ian stood still and tall, looking for all the world like he was completely calm. Jessie somehow doubted that was actually the case.

Peter said, "And they do this why?"

"Because they can."

And maybe to make a big brother proud.

CHAPTER TEN

I AN RELEASED THE lungful of breath he always held from the moment his youngest brother climbed onto the back of whatever bull he'd drawn until he was safely away from the bull, either on his own or with the help of the bull fighters. Alec appeared no worse the wear for being dumped onto his head.

As Ian watched Alec scramble up the metal arena railing even though Red Rum was trotting directly to the exit gate, it took another couple deep breaths to release the tension gripping his body. Regardless of how good of a bull rider Alec might become, the sport was inherently very dangerous. But it was what Alec wanted to do at this point in his life. Ian had to trust that with the mentorship of Bodie, a former top pro bull rider on the national tour, and everyone else tasked with keeping the riders safe—which included his bull fighting cousins—Alec would stay as safe as could be expected when bulls were involved. Even his sister was chipping in by learning to bull fight. Not what Ian would have chosen for her to do, but he had to trust Bodie to keep her safe. And Ian had no doubt Bodie would do it because he loved Caitlin.

Ian's gaze rose to the packed grandstands directly across the arena from where he stood above the bucking chutes. As if she'd snagged him with a lasso, he spotted Jessie Martin in the crowd. Or maybe he simply recognized his sister's hat still on Jessie's head.

Yeah, right. There had to be at least fifty women wearing damn near the same hat.

His gaze had immediately been caught by the silky black fall of long hair draped over one shoulder, her lush mouth spread in a wide smile directed at the dark-haired man seated next to her.

Ian planted his hands on his hips as his hackles instantly rose. Then he realized there was something familiar about the way the man sat. Like he had a stick up his butt. A federal agent stick. She was sitting next to her fellow agent, Peter Beck, in the grandstand. He was her partner, so of course she would be comfortable enough to smile like that at him.

What would it be like to have the full force of her smile, her real smile, turned on him again?

Why should he care? Especially considering the woman was insisting on including his family in her investigation.

The next cowboy slated to ride had drawn one of the Wright Ranch's bucking bulls, which Drew had named Cherry Bomb, so Ian remained on the raised platform to position and pull tight the flank strap after the rider nodded and the gate was pulled open.

But his focus wasn't what it normally was, with his gaze constantly flicking up toward the stands. He was nearly yanked over the chute rail when the gate opened and the bull broke for the arena because he didn't let go of the flank strap quickly enough. Luckily, Alec had returned to the platform to help his fellow rider set his bucking rope and was able to grab Ian's waistband and keep him from landing on his head in the chute.

"Holy crap, Ian," Alec exclaimed. "Are you okay? Did your hand get hung up?" His gaze dropped to Ian's gloved hands, probably looking for missing fingers.

"I'm fine, Alec. Thanks for the grab."

"Absolutely. No worries." It was clear Alec wasn't convinced Ian was fine judging from the way his baby brother was looking at him, like maybe he'd suffered a stroke or something.

Which meant he probably wasn't okay, he admitted when his attention drifted once again to where the FBI agents were seated. This time he found Beck watching him through a pair of binoculars. The prickling at the back of his neck began once again. But Jessie seemed to be watching the pickup riders herd Cherry Bomb, who seemed to be doing a victory lap after blowing up the bull rider who'd tried unsuccessfully to stick to him for more than a second, toward the exit.

"Is that Jessie?"

Ian turned and found Alec squinting toward the stands, having obviously followed where Ian had been looking.

"It is." Ian pulled his gloves off and shoved them into his back pocket as he stepped away from the bucking chutes. He headed for the stairs to make room for the stock contractors and bull riders working the next bulls.

"Who's that with her?" Alec asked, dogging his heels.

Pounding down the metal stairs, Ian considered telling his brother he didn't know who Peter was, but his stomach was already twisted up enough over the lies he'd told his family as it was. So he settled for, "He's a coworker of hers."

"Another forensic accounting lawyer from Portland? I heard there were two of them working at the sheriff's station." Alec was still right behind him, his spurs jangling.

Had they said she had come from Portland? Ian couldn't remember. He readjusted his hat and stopped, turning to face down Alec. "Yes. I don't know. Don't you have another ride?"

The kid grinned at him. "No, I don't. You're going to take her to the Chute Nine dance, right?"

"I have things to do—"

"We actually have hired hands—as in men who are paid, and paid well—to do the stuff you always insist on doing. Or watching them do it. You also have brothers." Alec pointed toward the stands. "That guy is clearly competition, Ian. You have to take her to the dance. Lock it down, bro." Alec hitched up his bull riding chaps in emphasis.

Ian pushed his hat up and considered his options. Everyone knew she was currently staying at his house. Not taking her to the dance named for a chute that didn't exist at the High Desert Rodeo grounds—there were only eight bucking chutes—might raise eyebrows. Especially considering it looked as though he would be expected to take her to Grant's daughter's wedding.

"She's beautiful, Ian. And according to Big Mike, she can stick a horse like a real pro."

Ian stilled. Big Mike must have seen Jessie successfully handle Chuck after the quail startled him after all.

"Don't let us down. Take her to the dance, man."

Ian blew out a frustrated breath. "She probably won't want to go."

Alec's face erupted in his infectious grin, creasing the filth on his face where the bull had made him eat dirt. "She will. Girls always want to dance. Especially with a cowboy."

"Keep telling yourself that, kid." But Ian knew the die was cast. For the first time in years he'd be taking a woman to the after-rodeo dance.

A woman who was already haunting him late at night.

"HE'S COMING THIS way," Peter said, gesturing with the paper cone containing the remnants of his shaved ice.

She didn't have to ask *he, who?* Because she knew without looking. Despite her best efforts to actually watch the rodeo, and the surprising amount of enjoyment doing so had given her, her attention kept straying to the big cowboy watching over those he cared about. Which pretty much included everyone.

And after the way her heart had lurched when he'd hung on to the big roan bull's flank strap a second too long, nearly getting himself yanked head over heels into the bull chute, she'd had the hardest time looking away.

"He walks like a storm trooper."

"No, he walks like a cowboy."

Peter lowered the shaved ice cone and sent her a quizzical look. "He isn't bow-legged."

"That's not—" She sighed. "Clearly you've never worn cowboy boots."

Peter snorted, crumpling the paper cone and setting it on the concrete between his feet. "Clearly."

She looked back at Ian as he followed the path she'd taken when she'd gone from the competitors' side of the rodeo grounds to the spectator side. He did not walk like a storm trooper, lock-step and following someone else's orders. He walked like a man who knew his worth. And from what she'd seen and heard today from the people who knew him, he was worth quite a lot.

Ian did not take long to reach them, despite slowing to acknowledge the people who greeted him. The somewhat grim set of his mouth ignited a spark of worry in her chest. Had Alec actually hurt himself when he'd been thrown from his bull? It was a struggle for Jessie to remain seated and not rush to meet him.

He made his way down their row and before he could sit down, Jessie asked, "Is Alec okay?"

Ian paused, his blond brows drawing together. "He's fine. Why?"

An unexpectedly strong sense of relief surged through her. "I thought—" She cut herself off. "Just wondering."

Ian's frown cleared and he seated himself next to her, immediately extending a hand to Peter. "How are you,

Peter?"

Peter shook his hand. "I'm good. Do you still have all your fingers?"

Ian glanced down at his fingers as he released Peter's hand, then obviously realized what Peter was referring to. "Oh. Yeah, I'm good."

Jessie asked, "What happened?"

He shrugged. "Didn't let go when I should have. I don't like to pull the flank strap tight too soon because that's what gets the bull bucking, and it can go real bad real fast if the gate hasn't opened all the way. It's all a matter of timing." He shrugged again, his gaze shifting to the arena, now filled with a riding club performing the closing routine.

Jessie studied his profile, noting the tightness of his jaw. Alec may not have been hurt, but something seemed off about Ian. If she wasn't convinced he was unflappable, she would think he was on edge.

Ian leaned forward to prop his elbows on his thighs, turned his gaze back to her, and asked, "What's the plan, now?"

Jessie said, "We continue our research"—meaning digging into the main players' finances—"and then you and I attend Grant Williams's daughter's wedding."

"No, I meant now. Tonight."

Peter stood. "I'm going back to the motel and go to bed. I think I'm having a sugar crash." He picked up the binocular case and the trash he'd accumulated at his feet. He met her gaze. "Let me know."

Which meant check in with him on regular intervals until she was snug in bed. "Yes, Dad."

As soon as Peter had cleared their row and begun his descent down the stadium stairs, Ian said, "Would you like to go to the Chute Nine dance?"

"The what?" She jerked her gaze back down to the arena, looking for a chute nine.

"There are only eight." Ian accurately guessed at her confusion. "They call the tent where the dance is held Chute Nine."

"Because you're supposed to burst out of it and let'er buck?"

His face softened a bit. "Or burst in. A lot of these cowboys don't get out much."

She laughed, then looked down at her not exactly dance-worthy outfit. "They are not alone. But don't you have animals to see to?"

He made a noise. "I have recently been reminded we actually pay people to do that sort of thing."

"And you have siblings . . ."

He gave an exaggerated nod. "I was reminded of that as well."

She smiled, imagining one of his younger brothers, probably Alec because he was just helping him, lecturing Ian on letting others handle a few things for a while. The guy really did need to learn how to let go.

"Would you like to go?"

She could absolutely muddle through a few line dances in the name of seeing, and possibly overhearing, who was talking to who. But she hesitated, trying to think what she'd packed that would be suitable to dance in.

"Usually pretty much everyone at least makes an appearance."

He almost sounded as if he was trying to entice her. Why? Her need to know had her saying, "Sure. I'd love to. But I'm not certain I packed the right thing to wear."

"What you are wearing right now is completely fine. This is a rodeo."

She looked around at the occasionally sparkly tops and equally sparkly jeans the women were wearing and the crisp, pristine, occasionally corporate logo festooned button-down shirts and dark-washed jeans worn by the men and thought he was giving rodeo a bad rap.

"If you're hungry, we can grab some food from one of the vendors and bring it in with us."

Jessie quickly glanced around her for the popcorn bag she'd emptied but was relieved to see that Peter had picked it up along with his garbage. She was about to decline, but realized he wouldn't have had the opportunity to snack on stadium fare like she had. He must be starving.

She instead said, "That would be great."

He stood and waited for her to rise before escorting her down the stadium stairs, through the concrete tunnel, and to the concourse where the food vendors were set up.

"What sounds good?"

She pulled in a lungful of incredible smells. One in particular stood out. "I can't remember the last time I had a hot dog."

His nod of approval was quick. "Hot dog it is."

They got in line at the hot dog stand, where several people approached Ian with congratulations on his animals' performances as well as that of his little brother. Each time he courteously introduced her as his friend, Jessie.

She started to like it. If only circumstances were different, she could see herself being friends with Ian Neisson.

Keeping her voice low, she said, "You know, I really thought the sheriff was exaggerating when he said you knew everyone."

"And I told you this is my community." He shrugged.

He ordered and paid for their hot dogs, chuckling in approval when she loaded hers with pretty much everything. But if she was going to have a hot dog, she was going to have a hot dog with the works.

Then he led her to the tent with a banner emblazoned with Chute Nine where the after-rodeo dance would be held.

The woman at the entrance taking tickets greeted them with wide eyes. "Ian! It's so nice to see you coming in here." She leaned in and stage-whispered, "Is this her? I heard she was pretty, but wow."

"Hey, Nancy. This is my friend, Jessie."

Maybe it was her imagination, but she thought he'd stopped emphasizing the word *friend*.

Jessie acknowledged the introduction then asked, "Where do we get tickets?"

Nancy waved her off. "Oh, you two don't need tickets. Just go on in and have fun."

"Thanks, Nancy," Ian said and ushered Jessie inside. He leaned close to say, "Sorry. Small town."

"It's no problem," she assured him, but found herself wondering if the small town, and its inherent gossip, was a problem for him?

Not liking how her pride started to itch at the thought, she reminded herself she needed to stay wary. This was an investigation, not a date. She followed his direction that led her to a vacant tall table in the far corner of the tent where they could stand and eat their hot dogs but still see the entirety of the space.

She was halfway through her laden hot dog when the band took to the stage and started playing an eclectic mix of popular country-western and classic rock music. Ian had polished off his dog in about three bites. He had been starving. And she supposed he had to fuel that big body somehow. While she ate Ian fetched a couple of beers that proved to be a great accompaniment to the dog.

The music was good and made for easy toe tapping while she finished her food. But it was also too loud to allow for much talking, let alone overhearing anything useful.

As a result, she found herself accepting Ian's offer to dance. She expected a lot of spinning and twirling, but instead he pulled her close, leading her into a slow two-step that completely emptied her brain of rational thought.

Ian's grip engulfed hers, his ranch-roughened skin warm against her palm. His other hand rested in what was becoming a very familiar spot on the small of her back, his long fingers splayed. She'd automatically reached up and settled her free hand on his muscular shoulder, her fingers flexing into him of their own volition.

At first, they'd started out with several inches between them, but with each synchronized step they drew closer, inch by inch, until her breasts touched his hot chest and their bellies and hips pressed together.

She'd intended to scan the tent as they moved around the dance floor, but she couldn't pull her gaze from his blue eyes, bottomless in the dim light of the tent. He was sucking her in to his aura of strength and care and her wariness was proving to be a thin shield.

Needing to break the tension mounting between them, she tossed out a very old joke. "Is that your belt buckle or are you just happy to be dancing with me?"

Only one corner of his mouth tipped up. "I'm not wearing a belt."

She missed a step, and he pulled her closer still to steady her.

The song ended, but he continued to hold her.

The part of her brain that had been running her life for the past ten years, keeping her safe from heartache, screamed at her to step away, to try a different tack to get back to the life she'd planned for herself.

But the music started up again, this time a true slow ballad that spoke of the hope of love, and Ian—or maybe it was her—started them moving again, flowing with the music and whatever it was that was pulsing between them. A voice in her head said she knew exactly what *it* was, but she shied away from naming it.

Instead she allowed herself some grace. She allowed herself this moment. Just this moment. With this man, in a dim tent at a small-town rodeo. She'd get back on her solitary track soon enough.

She had no idea how long she and Ian danced, always a slow, easy two-step regardless of the pace of the song. But when the band announced they would be taking a break, she felt as if she'd woken from a very long, very wonderful dream.

Ian smiled at her and stepped back, but kept hold of her hand and only slid his other hand from her back to rest lightly on her hip bone. "Is it hot in here? I'm hot. Are you hot?"

She laughed and nodded, her throat too tight to allow for speech.

"Would you like another beer? Or something else to drink? Or we could get some air—"

"Air. Yes. Can we go for a walk?"

"Absolutely." He released her hip, but kept hold of her hand to lead her toward the exit.

It was only then that Jessie realized how many people were watching the two of them, their smiles wide and encouraging or sweetly indulgent.

The attention directed her and Ian's way should have been like a bucket of cold water over her head, but instead warmth unfurled within her at the proof of how well liked and cared for Ian was.

And it was her hand he was holding.

And it was her heart at risk of breaking.

CHAPTER ELEVEN

J ESSIE STROLLED WITH Ian among the competitors' trailers, campers, RVs, and animal pens beneath the ridiculous abundance of stars filling the cloudless sky, her hand tucked safely within his. She appreciated the coolness of the night air, a welcome contrast to how hot he'd made her. But why did she think her hand was safe in his? She didn't need a big, strong cowboy to make her feel safe in the dark. She had a holstered gun in her cowboy boot, for god's sake.

She had nothing to fear at the High Desert rodeo grounds. It seemed as if most of the owners of the recreational vehicles were either at the dance, already snug inside their rigs, or tending to their animals.

But the way Ian held her hand—secure but not tight, enveloped but not smothered—unfurled a feeling of safety within her. Maybe even contentment. Whatever it was, it was warm and very, very foreign.

And she felt the shield of wariness that she'd counted on to protect her for a decade crack.

She glanced at Ian's handsome profile. The crown of his hat was illuminated by the warm glow of the temporary lighting set up at regular intervals throughout the traveling competitors' village, but most of his face remained in shadow. Utterly unreadable.

Normally silence didn't bother her, but tonight she couldn't bear it. She mused, "It's been a long time since I danced." She stopped herself from saying *like that*. Barely.

He looked down at her, and she made herself look up at the stars, as if the blanket of sparkling pinpricks of light could compare to the glow of heat in his dark blue eyes.

"It's been a long time since I danced like *that*."

His voicing her thoughts sent a shiver skipping over her skin. Maybe it was the beer, or maybe just the starlight, but she succumbed to the dare to skirt close to the fire of her attraction to Ian Neisson. "Like what?"

He stopped just outside the pool of light created by the nearest temporary light pole and turned to face her. Drawing their joined hands to his side, he gently forced her to take a step closer to him. The heat pulsing off his muscular body was more pronounced in the crisp, high desert air. Excitement shimmied over her. Was he going to kiss her? Good lord, did she want him to?

Easing his hat back off his brow, he said, "Like I never wanted to stop."

She swallowed hard to clear her throat. "Before tonight, I can honestly say I have never danced like *that*."

"I'm sorry," he said in a low, gruff voice.

The sincerity in his tone stripped her of her usual artifice. "I'm not. It makes what happened in there"—she tipped her head toward the Chute Nine tent—"that much better."

She was definitely too close to the fire now.

He edged a little closer, his boots scuffing in the packed dirt, until they were standing almost as close as they had been while dancing. "I have a hard time believing that no man has ever held you close and moved you across the dance floor. You are a beautiful woman, Jessie. I have a hard time believing no one else has noticed."

His praise made her uncomfortable. Yet a thrill of delight rocketed through her veins. Unexpected. Scary.

"What's wrong?"

She realized she'd taken a step back. "I'm just not great with compliments."

His eyebrows shot up.

The darkness made a confession, of sorts, easier. "My stepdad always made me feel bad about my looks, harping on the fact that I would never be taken seriously, no matter what I ended up doing, because of the way I looked."

The FBI had taught her that her physical attributes were a tool, an asset, a weapon, even, to be used to achieve her goals. Considering she was standing here with Ian because of her job, she kept that lesson to herself.

And she realized she no longer wanted to use that particular weapon to get what she wanted from Ian. Because she actually liked him. Liked and admired him. Despite the fact he was a cowboy. Something she'd never thought possible after Devin, a cowboy through and through, had so completely broken her heart.

He grew still. "Do you look like your mom?"

"A little. I can't say whether or not I favor my biological dad because I've never met him or any of his family." Her mother had insisted they weren't worth meeting. The fact that they had never tried to contact Jessie had reinforced her mother's opinion.

"You never had any desire to track him down?" Obviously, he was thinking of the resources available to her through her job. Not to mention the close relationship he had with his own family. She could imagine Ian having a hard time wrapping his mind around someone not wanting to be a part of a close relative's life. His entire world was steeped in legacy, land, and family. He would never be able to understand what had shaped her, let alone her determination to shake off her previous life by reinventing herself.

His familial relationships were just as foreign to her. She firmly believed blind reliance on family made a person weak. Her mother had chosen not just one, but two men with zero desire to be a father to, let alone love, Jessie.

"No. No desire whatsoever. My mom swears he knew about her pregnancy but didn't want to be involved. As much as it pisses me off, I've decided to do the grown-up thing by choosing to respect that."

His free hand drifted up to snag a lock of her hair from her shoulder, sliding it through his fingers. The motion was as erotic to her as his actually caressing her skin would be. "And you feel lost because of it."

"No," she practically croaked. She cleared her throat and tried again. "No. That's not it."

Clearly Ian thought she was holding herself back because of daddy issues. Sure, her daddy issues had driven her into the arms of the first cowboy who'd shown her real attention.

"We had a hand who promised me—" She cut herself off. She'd never spoken of her heartbreak because it was something that had happened to a foolish girl in the past. She was no longer that girl.

"He promised you . . ." he prompted, obviously not willing to let the matter slide.

"The moon and the stars. Then promptly split for parts unknown after he'd gotten what he wanted from me. And he took my horse with him."

Ian pulled his chin back. "He stole your horse?"

"Worse. My stepfather sold her to him behind my back."

"They broke your heart."

She shrugged, trying to minimize the hurt, the revelation.

Ian slipped his hand from her hair to the side of her neck. "Heartbreak is harder to bear without the support of family."

He'd nailed it on the head. She'd felt alone, abandoned after Devin had seduced her then kicked her to the proverbial curb and took off with her horse. She'd been unable to tell her mom or friends what had happened because she didn't want to be perceived as weak or needy. Instead, she'd just seemed stupid for letting him take so much from her.

She shrugged it off. "Not if you're strong enough."

Ian released her hand so he could bring both of his hands up to cup her face. "No one should ever have to be that strong."

But she *was* that strong. Even without the badge or the gun or the hand-to-hand fighting skills that earned her the respect she'd longed for in her teens. Being alone had tempered her like nothing else could.

Ian's hands dropped away from her and she realized she'd taken another step back from him. Shit. The crack in her shield was showing. He scared her on a level she couldn't fathom.

He hooked his thumbs in the front pocket of his jeans. He wasn't going to crowd her. Or force her to accept his comfort. Always the gentleman.

Damn cowboy.

The crack in her shield widened.

He toed the dirt with his boot. "You're definitely stronger than me. I would be lost without my family."

She blinked at his admission of weakness. And melted more than a little inside. "From what I've heard from the community and seen with my own eyes, your family would be lost without you. You're the one who takes care of everyone else, Ian. It takes a lot of strength to put others first to the degree you do."

His gaze dropped to the tips of his boots, the brim of his hat hiding his face from her. "It's not strength. It's commitment. When I came home after my mom's accident—"

She regained the step she'd taken and gripped his forearm until he looked up at her. "It wasn't an accident, Ian. It was a criminal act. Karl Fletcher released your grandfather's bull into the corral your mom and sister were in, after using a cattle prod on him, to conceal the theft he was committing."

"You're right. But it doesn't change what came after. My

grandfather withdrew into the business of the ranch and my father—well, my father just flat-out withdrew. He loved her so much." He pulled in a breath.

Jessie's heart, jaded as it was, nearly broke.

"My mom needed me to be there for my brothers and sister, and for the ranch she loved. I threw myself into doing that for her even before she made me vow to take care of them—at the end—when she knew her time was almost up. Granted, she also made me promise to keep the wood elves from beating up the barn fairies . . ." He shook his head and rubbed his eyes with his thumb and index finger of his free hand. "She was pretty out of it at the end."

Jessie's protective shield broke completely in two. She had never wanted to wrap her arms around a man's waist and hold tight more in her entire life.

She settled for giving his forearm another squeeze. "I'm so sorry, Ian." There was nothing else she could say. How could she even go about comforting a strong, incredibly capable man who'd just revealed his inner pain? A pain that possibly explained a lot. "Is that why you've never been in a serious relationship?"

He shrugged, very unconvincingly. "Maybe. Needless to say, my family is very important to me."

She'd love to say she understood, that she could relate, but she couldn't. Because she didn't. Except for the self-deprivation part. She had never had anyone choose her over what they personally wanted from life, nor had she ever had anyone want the same from her. Outside of the bureau, that is. Her peers were her family, of sorts. She released his forearm and stepped back.

Ian was watching her with an intensity she could feel more than see in the dim light.

She heard him pull in a deep breath then release it noisily. "Look, Jess—"

His use of the nickname melted something inside of her.

"I know you're working, but—"

"I'm not working. Not right now." A total lie. Her job was twenty-four-seven. But she realized with a flash of clarity she didn't want to be working right now. Not tonight. Not here, with this man. She pulled his sister's cowboy hat from her head and ran a hand through her mashed hair.

He shifted his weight. Toward her? Or had she closed the space between them?

"Is an FBI special agent ever not working?" he asked softly.

Busted.

Still holding the hat in her hand, she spread her hands and shrugged, unable to contain her guilt.

He brought a hand up to cup her cheek. "It's okay, Jess. You are committed to your job as much as I am to my family. Your job is your family."

She blinked up at him. How could he perceive her inner thoughts so well? His ability to do so should send her running for the hills. Instead she shifted closer. What was it about this man that got to her so?

"I'm so glad you have that. And I really admire your commitment." He shifted toward her yet again, drawing her in with his words, his heat. "I knew the second I met you that you were a badass, and you proved it by being there for me by snapping up Karl Fletcher after he went after my sister. Again."

There was nothing badass about throwing the weight of the law at a man who'd tried to murder a woman and her child by setting an enraged bull loose on them, and then tried again to finish the job years later. It had been a very gratifying moment for her.

"Not to mention when you found Amanda's stolen horse so quickly."

The respect and admiration in his tone had her cheeks flaming. His words were more intoxicating than any drug.

"Don't ever, ever apologize for being committed to your job." His other hand came up to hold her face too. "Don't ever apologize for being you."

Jessie gripped Ian's waist, crushing the hat in her hand, popped up onto her tiptoes, and kissed him. There really was no other response she could give such an amazing man after he'd said the most wonderful thing that could be said to her.

He deepened the kiss, his lips firm, his tongue hot, and his fingers flexing gently against her jaw before sliding back into her hair. She melted against him, his hardness fitting perfectly against her softness. Her body was on fire. An ache for more pulsed through her. Need, attraction, and daring urged her closer still. She clung to him with every fiber of her being. Why couldn't she have just this one moment, here, with him?

Because she was an FBI agent working an investigation, that was why. An investigation Ian Neisson might be involved in.

No. She'd barely formed the thought before she rejected it with everything in her. But ingrained habits of self-preservation were hard to break.

In her case, impossible, and her heart folded in on itself.

IAN COULD FEEL Jessie's withdrawal even before she broke off their kiss and stepped away from him. Her mouth had grown less receptive, her grip on his hips had relaxed. Her skin cooled beneath his hands.

Thank god one of them had some common sense.

Every ounce of his common sense had fled like a puff of smoke in a gale when she'd first grabbed hold of his waist and rose up on her tiptoes to kiss him, her mouth as hot and lush as he'd imagined it would be all the times he'd thought about it.

Like after seeing her pleasure from returning Whiskey Throttle to Amanda.

And after seeing her settle Chuck when the quail startled him.

And while watching her eat the apple he'd brought with them as they sat beneath his favorite aspen tree.

And when she'd risen from the hot tub, her water-soaked tank top and shorts clingy and dripping, her glistening skin flushed from the heat of the tub.

Ian had hoped holding her close against him on the dance floor, moving with her to the music their connection seemed to create, would be enough to quell the ache to kiss her. As Jess would say, he'd been wrong. So wrong.

His entire body was still hot and hard with the memory of her body pressed against his.

He resettled his hat on his head and watched her move steadily, purposefully away from him. She fiddled with Caitlin's hat between her hands, and he realized Jess had mashed it when she'd gripped his hips. His stomach clenched as he remembered the sensation. She'd nearly popped his own hat clean off his head when she'd grabbed hold of him like that.

He wanted her to do it again.

Tilting his head back to the stars, he resolutely crushed the want. As well as the longing burning in his chest. He had to keep his family's reputation above reproach, and sleeping with one of the investigating agents wasn't the way to do it.

Sleeping with the investigating agent?

His subconscious had escalated that quickly. They had only kissed.

But who was he kidding? He looked back at Special Agent Jessica Martin. Of course he wanted to sleep with her. He had since the moment he'd recognized that she was the one in charge.

And now that he knew what drove her . . . He wanted her even more. He wanted to sooth the hurt left by an uncaring family, to assure her that not every cowboy was a user.

But it couldn't happen.

As soon as she caught the cattle rustlers working the ION

territory—and she would catch the thieving bastards, he had no doubt—she would return to the big city and its big crime. And continue on her quest to shove everything that had hurt her on her family's ranch deep into a box she would never have to open ever again.

Having returned Caitlin's cowboy hat to its proper form, Jessie put it back on her head and turned to face him. "I'm sorry, Ian. That was . . . That wasn't cool. I should never have kissed you."

No way was she shouldering the blame. "In case you didn't notice, I kissed you back."

She waved his complicity off, as if he couldn't be expected to control himself.

Like hell. He'd been doing a hell of a job controlling himself for the past ten years.

Sure, no other woman he'd encountered in that time had tested him like she had, but still . . .

She raised her chin, as if mustering her resolve. "Will you still take me to Grant Williams's daughter's wedding?"

"Lillian."

"What?"

He moved close enough to her that he could repair the crease in the crown of Caitlin's hat, gently using his fingertips to push the felt back down. "Grant Williams's daughter's name is Lillian. If you're going to attend her wedding, you should at least know her name."

"So you'll still take me?"

"Why wouldn't I?"

"Because I—" Her gaze dropped to his mouth and his

stomach clenched hard again. "Because I kissed you."

"I can think of a whole hell of a lot of other worse things that you could have done to me. And don't forget I kissed you back. We've covered this." He stepped back so his brain would work. "I still intend to help you find the assholes who are stealing from my neighbors and working with the firebug who stole Amanda's horse as well as that bastard Fletch. I'm sorry I crossed the line—"

"I'm the one who kis—"

He held up a hand to stop her. "I crossed the line, and I apologize. But let's just get through this. Agreed?"

She hesitated, her gaze searching his.

It took all his grit not to blink.

"Agreed," she finally said. "I'll understand completely if you want me to go back to the hotel."

Like hell. The thought of not having her close by sent a strange sort of panic through his veins. He didn't care why. He simply knew he wasn't letting her go yet.

He snagged her elbow and started them toward where he had parked his truck next to the other Wright Ranch trailers and vehicles. "No. Everyone already knows you are staying with me at the ranch. Which you should still do. Especially if we are going to go to Lillian's wedding together, as expected."

Despite . . . everything, his hand slipped down her arm to her hand and his fingers twinned with hers as if they had walked hand-in-hand for years. The contact created an unfamiliar ache deep in his heart. An ache he'd just as soon not experience, but he had no intention of letting go.

They walked holding hands through the rows of camper trailers, RVs, and livestock trailers that had popped up for the rodeo. Ian refused to think about how right her hand felt in his and how he dreaded letting go.

But some things just weren't meant to be.

CHAPTER TWELVE

SITTING CROSS-LEGGED IN the middle of the beautifully appointed guest bed in the Wright Ranch's manager house—Ian's house—with her laptop in front of her, Jessie tipped her head back and stared at the ceiling. She couldn't focus.

Let's just get through this.

Yes, let's.

Ever since she and Ian had returned from the rodeo grounds and immediately bade each other an awkward good night, Jessie had been replaying what they had said to each other under the stars.

After she'd kissed him.

Jessie covered her face with her hands and flopped back onto the stack of pillows behind her. Why had she kissed him?

Because he was gorgeous, smart, steadfast, kind, and—well, gorgeous.

Not to mention a cowboy.

She groaned and flung her hands out to her sides. She had kissed Ian Neisson and he had kissed her back. Oh, had he kissed her back. Her lips still tingled from the press of his, the mere memory of the touch of his tongue on hers set off a storm low in her belly. She'd known from the second she'd met his deep blue gaze across the interrogation table that she was attracted to him, but she'd had no idea just how strong the attraction would be.

Until that kiss.

A toe-curling, mind-blowing kiss that scared the crap out of her.

Let's just get through this.

"Yes, let's," she muttered to herself and shoved herself back upright to stare once again at the spreadsheet displayed on her computer screen. She had to get a grip. She was on the clock. Doing a job with a purpose. And she couldn't let anything, or anyone, derail her plans for the future.

When Jessie had called Peter to check in after their return to the ranch she had asked him to send her the latest livestock sales report he'd procured from the state's department of agriculture. There was no way she'd be falling asleep anytime soon, so she might as well work. And the more hard facts and figures she knew cold, the easier it would be to steer conversations or pick out pertinent information she might overhear at Lillian's wedding and reception.

But the columns of ear tag numbers and brand inspection verifications kept blurring, replaced by intense blue eyes and the heart pounding feel of his belly against hers.

She considered sneaking into Ian's office and riffling through his files, but immediately rejected the idea. She couldn't violate Ian that way. And not just because of the way his mouth felt on hers. He was a good man. An honorable man.

The sort of man who kept promises to a dead mother.

A door creaked somewhere down the hall from her room and Jessie froze. Listening hard, she tracked the sound of what could only be bare feet padding down the slate floor. The footsteps stopped outside her door.

Jessie almost reached for the bedside lamp to turn out the light, but realized it was undoubtedly the glow of light from beneath her door that had stopped Ian in the first place. She waited, afraid to breathe.

After what seemed a lifetime, she heard him pad away. The snick of the refrigerator opening, the clink of glass—was he getting a beer?—let her know he'd gone to the kitchen, then she heard him head back into the hall. And stop outside her door again. In the truck on the way back from the rodeo she'd felt him pulling away, distancing himself from her. Had he changed his mind about taking her to the wedding?

Or was he simply bringing her a beer too? God, she hoped so. No wait, she didn't. Because then he would have to knock on her door, and she would let him in, all barefoot and bare . . .

No. She didn't want a beer.

The sound of him continuing down the hall and closing his bedroom door reached her.

Jessie's heart thumped hard in her chest and the longing he'd ignited clogged her throat. The disappointment washing over her was totally uncalled for, but undeniable.

Let's just get through this.

Yes, let's.

IAN TRIED TO keep his distance from Special Agent Jessica Martin. He really did—despite his middle-of-the-night trips to the kitchen that gave him the chance to lurk outside her door and discover that she was having as much difficulty sleeping as he was. Her light had remained on well into the night but was off when he was leaving to complete his usual morning routine, which made him believe she wasn't simply falling asleep with her light on. And Jessie didn't strike him as the afraid of the dark type.

When he'd returned to the house the morning after they'd attended the rodeo, he'd found her sliding her laptop computer into her tote bag. She asked him to take her into town so she could check in with Special Agent Beck and the sheriff, and maybe do a little shopping for something to wear to Lillian's wedding.

The image of her undressing behind nothing more than a curtain at Pineville's lone dress boutique had him tossing her the keys to his truck. No way could he wait on the other side of that dressing room curtain and not go up in flames.

He didn't see her again until that evening, when he walked through the sliding glass door and found her deveining shrimp she'd purchased in the hopes he'd grill a little surf to go with the endless supply of turf he had in his fridge and freezer.

While he always had the big house to go to if he wanted to eat with someone, walking into his own kitchen to find someone . . . Who was he kidding? Jessie wasn't just someone. With her gleaming fall of black hair, flashing green eyes, and quick mind, she was his fantasy come to life.

Allowing himself the indulgence of an evening with her, he'd barbequed the shrimp and some steak while she made a salad. They'd eaten on the patio, talking about horses—which she actually knew quite a lot about—and watching the sun set behind the mountains.

He almost—almost—asked her if she wanted to enjoy the hot tub, but unlike most guys around these parts, he had not been kicked in the head. Instead they said their good nights and retreated into their respective rooms.

The next morning he didn't see her at all. The keys to the truck he'd given her free use of were gone, so he assumed she'd returned to town to either work or shop. Possibly both.

He was useless the rest of the day, his mind constantly drifting to what Jess might be doing. Imagining her busy with police work he could handle. But the thoughts of her trying on dresses, or heaven help him, low cut and fitted pantsuits, had him leaving a funnel chute gate open.

"Hey!" Big Mike hollered, scrambling up on the corral fencing to escape the steers Ian had accidentally allowed loose.

"Shit. Sorry, Mike." Ian mounted Clint and set to work rounding up the cattle he'd allowed out. Unfortunately, they were the steers used for steer wrestling and roping, chosen for their quickness and agility. And despite having a topnotch cutting horse beneath him, Ian's focus wasn't what it should have been.

By the time Ian had the last steer wrangled Big Mike was

laughing hysterically. "Boss, you are so twitterpated."

"What?"

He hopped down from the corral fencing. "You know where the baby forest animals meet their mates and start—"

"I know, Big Mike." Ian angled Clint so he could close the corral gate after the last steer. "And I am not twitterpated."

"How could you not be? That girl is beautiful."

"She's not a girl, Mike. You seriously need to get out more." Jess was a woman and so much more.

"You are not wrong, Boss. On either count."

"That's my job, Big Mike."

"Where is she, anyhow? Because I'm pretty sure she could have had those steers corralled in half the time."

"Now *you* are not wrong. The woman has skills." One of which, it seemed, was wrapping him around her little finger. He almost told Mike that Jess was working, but he caught himself just in time. "She's shopping. For something to wear to the wedding this weekend."

"Lillian's?"

Ian dismounted. "Yep."

Big Mike came to take hold of Clint's bridle. "Hopefully this one will stick."

"That's exactly what Grant said."

Scrubbing the big palomino's neck, Mike said, "I'll take care of this guy. Why don't you go see if your gal is back from town."

Without hesitation Ian said, "Thanks, Big Mike," and handed over the reins.

"No worries, Boss."

Ian was already on the crushed gravel path leading to his house before he remembered he was supposed to be distancing himself from Jessie. Well, shit. It was too late now. And the closer he came to his house the faster his heart beat. The sensible part of his brain told him to turn right back around and find something else to do until dark. Unfortunately, that part was being noisily overwhelmed by the rest of his brain, not to mention all of his body, that was clamoring for any sort of interaction with Jessie.

As he stepped through the sliding door Jessie was setting down her tote and a large bag from a store he didn't recognize on the kitchen bar.

"Where did you go?"

She turned and gave him an adorably guilty look. "I drove to Bend. I hope you don't mind."

"Of course not." He wasn't surprised at all that she'd had to make the roughly one-hour drive to the largest city in the high desert.

"And Ian?"

He paused in the act of toeing off his boots. "Yeah?"

"I really like driving that truck."

He barked out a laugh. "Anytime, Jess. Anytime." She may have taken herself out of the country, but the country was still firmly in her. The bloom of admiration for Jessie broadsided Ian. He shoved it aside with the same determination he'd used for the past ten years. He pointed to the shopping bag. "I'm sorry you had to drive so far, but it looks like you were successful?"

She smiled broadly, and he decided he'd have to amend his quip about having never been kicked in the head.

"I was."

"Show me?"

"Nope. You'll have to wait until tomorrow." From the shopping bag she pulled out a small cream and lavender wrapped gift box. "I also bought a wedding present for the bride and groom."

Ian raised his eyebrows.

"It's just a crystal candy dish." She shrugged in a *what else do you give people you don't know* way. "And I got you something too." She winked, and this time he felt the impact of her pleasure in his gut.

"What?"

She wagged a playful finger. "Tomorrow. I also picked up a fire roasted chicken for dinner. Just on the off chance you were tired of beef."

Her thoughtfulness was a vise around his chest, squeezing the air from his lungs.

It took him a minute to be able to say, "Thank you. Chicken sounds awesome."

The evening wasn't as warm as it had been the night before, so they decided to keep things simple and eat at the breakfast bar, side by side and companionable. He knew he should question her about the investigation, but telling her about the steers he'd accidentally let loose—minus the part about him being distracted by thoughts of her—was a lot more pleasurable.

Especially because the story made her laugh, and Ian decided he hadn't heard a better sound. Ever.

They cleaned up their dishes, side by side, chatting about the wiliness of steers and the pluses and minuses of a good cutting horse. And while her laugh might have been the best sound he'd ever heard, hearing her say good night to him at the guest room door, turned out to be the worst.

Because now all he could think about was kissing her again.

And he was aching for so much more.

JESSIE DALLIED AS much as she dared in her en suite bathroom, but the wedding was scheduled at eleven—a consolation to those who needed to attend the rodeo later, either as stock contractors or competitors.

Normally she didn't angst over what she wore or how she looked because she usually thought of both as tools. Means to an end.

But this morning all she could think about was whether or not Ian would think she looked pretty in the pale green summer dress she'd bought in the fifth boutique she'd visited the day before. She suffered the same indecision over her hair. Up? Down? Braided? Loose?

Remembering how Ian had captured a strand of her hair and caressed it between his fingertips, she decided to leave her hair loose, but added a few curls with a hot iron in consideration of the gravity of the day's event. The only jewelry she wore was her tiny gold horseshoe necklace.

When the enticing scent of coffee seeped beneath the door and she heard what sounded like Ian emptying the dishwasher, an act of nervous energy if there ever was one, she knew it was time to leave her room. She checked for the second time that the tiny recorder, her official ID, smallest firearm, and most importantly—considering the threats of the day—her lipstick were safely tucked into the small clutch she'd bought to complement her new dress. Grabbing the wedding gift in one hand and tucking the tissue-wrapped gift she'd also purchased for Ian under her arm, she girded her loins and left the safety of the guest room.

She closed the door behind her as softly as she could, but when she rounded the wall between the hall and the kitchen she saw that Ian had stopped what he was doing, obviously having heard her. He was wearing a tan suede western-cut blazer, a white button-down shirt with a bolo tie, sharply creased black slacks, and shiny black cowboy boots that had clearly never seen anything resembling manure. His light tan felt cowboy hat sat on the breakfast bar.

Her step faltered. Ian was as attractive to her all spiffed up as he was while sitting in the saddle. Great. Just great.

At the sight of her, the coffee cup in his hand swung loose, suspended by its handle.

"Good morning," she said, a smile tugging at the corners of her mouth as she set the wedding gift on the breakfast bar.

He coughed and fumbled to set the coffee cup on the counter. "Good morning."

Her self-consciousness over her choice of dress skyrocketing, she shifted her clutch from hand to hand. When he continued to simply stare at her, she glanced down at the modest skirt of the dress she'd initially thought would be perfect for an early wedding on a ranch. "Is this okay?" She'd been going for classy and understated, but maybe she'd missed the mark.

"That dress is more than okay. It's perfect. And your hair is beautiful."

She had to grip tight to her clutch with both hands to keep from reaching up to touch her hair. "Thank you. It was a struggle to find this dress."

"It was a battle well fought." He took a step toward her then seemed to stop himself. "Would you like some coffee? A muffin?"

"Just coffee would be great."

"Sit down and I'll get it. Easy enough when you drink it black."

The fact that he had not only noticed, but remembered how she liked her coffee, sent a ridiculous flush of pleasure through her. She pulled the tissue-wrapped gift from beneath her arm. "I got you something too."

He stopped with the coffee carafe hovering over a mug. "You didn't have to."

"I know. That's what makes it fun." She held out the gift to him.

Ian set the carafe and cup down and stepped close enough to take the parcel from her. He pulled the store's logo sticker loose from the tissue and opened the folds. He laughed. "A belt." He lifted the tooled black leather belt by the large, horse-embossed silver buckle and inspected it.

"You know, because the other night—"

"I get it." He laughed again, and the glint in his eye made her think he was remembering what she had jokingly mistaken for his belt buckle.

Jessie's cheeks grew warm as she took a seat at the breakfast bar. "What time do we have to leave?"

Ian finished pouring her coffee and set the steaming mug in front of her, then unbuckled the dress belt he wore and pulled it from his pants' loops. "The Bar W is almost an hour east of here. So we have more than enough time for at least a cup of coffee." He replaced his belt with the one she'd bought him, grinning at the perfect fit.

Judging by the nervous energy pinging through her veins, the last thing Jessie needed was a cup of coffee, but she didn't want to tip off Ian to how nervous she was. Because it was ridiculous that she was nervous at all. It wasn't as if she would be the center of attention. Nor was this going to be a takedown. She was simply attending a function hosted by a person of interest in her current investigation. To see what she could see, hear what she might hear.

Granted, she and Peter had determined the logistics of the Bar W made remote monitoring and recording impossible, so she had her recorder in her purse to corroborate anything of importance she might hear. And she truly didn't believe she would be in any sort of danger.

Not on the arm of Ian Neisson.

She blinked at the thought, and realized he was staring at her.

She downed her coffee in a couple of gulps. "Shall we?"

"Like I said, we have time to drink our coffee, not inhale it."

"I know, but I'd prefer to arrive early."

"To snoop?"

She didn't detect any sarcasm in his tone. "To get the lay of the land."

"I hate to break it to you, but you're not going to find anything out of the ordinary at Grant's ranch. The Bar W is pretty similar to the Wright Ranch."

"And I hate to break it to you, but the Wright Ranch, and anything similar, is far outside the realm of ordinary."

Ian saluted her with his coffee mug, then downed its contents as she had hers. Setting the now empty cup on the counter, he said, "Then we shall." He snagged his hat from the counter and rounded the breakfast bar, offering her his elbow.

She smiled her thanks into his blue eyes.

"You really do look lovely."

There was nothing else she could say besides a simple, "Thank you."

His broad smile said it was enough.

THOUGH HE'D MADE himself stop glancing toward Jessie every minute because he didn't want her to think he was creeping on her, Ian was very aware of Jessie as she chatted with the cattlemen's association official he'd just introduced her to at the reception. And not because of the heightened interest that practically pulsed off her every time he introduced her to someone who could be of use to her investigation.

Ian freely admitted that keeping his gaze from being glued on her was proving incredibly difficult because she flat-out mesmerized him. Not because of her beauty. He'd accepted that weeks ago. But because today he'd seen her normal aura of confidence fail her. She'd been uncertain, which had endeared her in a way nothing else could.

The music started, and Ian asked her to dance. He didn't even consider that he could be interrupting what might be an important conversation for her. All that mattered was that he get her in his arms again while he could.

She smiled an apology to the man she was talking with and allowed Ian to whisk her off to the dance floor.

"That was some wedding."

Thankfully, she didn't sound perturbed that he'd interrupted her. "I guess if you're going to do it three times, you might as well do it how you want."

"Still, bongos were a bold choice."

"They were. Indeed they were." He chuckled and reflexively drew her closer. She fit so perfectly against him, moved so effortlessly with him, it was easy to stop thinking and just *feel*.

Jessie tucked her face against his neck as if she'd been made for the spot. "Today was good," she said softly. "I learned a lot. I'm not entirely sure how much, if anything, is useful, but it's better than a poke in the eye."

"What?" He drew back to look at her. "A poke in the eye?"

She grinned. "Well it is."

He laughed. "A lot of things are."

"Exactly." She blinked sweetly up at him.

Where they were, who was around them, faded away. Nothing registered in his brain except for the welcoming warmth in her beautiful green eyes and the happy tilt of her full, red lips. Ian was drawn to her like a starving horse to sweet spring grass.

The next thing he knew he was kissing Special Agent Jessica Martin. Right there on the dance floor. In front of family and friends.

And she was kissing him back.

Again.

CHAPTER THIRTEEN

J ESSIE OPENED TO Ian as he deepened the kiss, her hand sliding from where it had rested on the top of his shoulder while they danced to the nape of his hot, strong neck. His mouth was like a lead line, drawing her up against him from her very core. His lips slid gently, then more persistently, over hers as he kissed her. He tasted so good. Like expensive champagne and her closest held fantasies.

"Atta boy, Ian," someone said behind her.

She jerked away from him.

Ian loosened his hold on her slightly, his blue gaze searching hers. "Kinda forgot where we were."

"Me too." She could kid herself into believing she'd kissed him on a dance floor in front of at least a dozen witnesses simply to reinforce her cover. But that would be a lie. A lie she didn't want to tell because for once she'd done something for herself, allowed herself something that wasn't to somehow benefit her job.

"Sorry."

She shook her head. "Don't be." She meant it. She had no idea what was developing between her and Ian, but it was definitely mutual. It was a miracle no one had told them to get a room.

Jessie's face flamed. If they'd been alone their kiss would have progressed to something else. Something she was starting to believe she wanted.

She glanced around the temporary dance floor that had been set up just beyond the stone patio behind Grant Williams's huge house. Where Thomas Wright had gone more for the northwest resort lodge look when he'd built his home, Grant had definitely drawn inspiration from the dynasty ranch house look. The DJ was playing a popular song that had drawn a large number of the wedding attendees out onto the dance floor, and luckily it seemed most of the dancers were more concerned with getting their groove on than paying attention to what she and Ian had been doing.

Then her gaze collided with Thomas Wright's. He was standing off to the side of the dance floor with a group of fellow ranchers including Ian's father, a glass tumbler containing some dark liquor in his hand. He dropped his chin and raised his glass slightly in what she thought might be a salute of approval. Or maybe a warning?

Ian's hand on her waist flexed in clear reassurance.

She looked back up at him and found him watching her. Did he not care what anyone thought of them being together?

But his friends and family didn't know the truth of their relationship. That she had basically blackmailed Ian into helping her, using his dedication to his family and neighbors to get his cooperation.

But he knew, and he'd still kissed her. Twice. She was afraid to consider what his kiss might mean.

His fingers flexed against her again, only this time he drew her closer. "What do you think about getting out of here?"

She hesitated. She was supposed to be working.

He leaned down to speak next to her ear, his lips brushing her hair. "Do you still need to talk to someone? Didn't you get what you wanted from Grant?"

What she got from Grant Williams had been a lot of complaining about how much his daughter's quest for true love was costing him. That at thirty-nine, Lillian had married and divorced twice before, and seemed to think this third time would be the charm. Though Jessie hadn't had the opportunity to meet the bride and her much younger groom, they appeared to be in love as they'd stood beneath the flower-drenched arch and exchanged their vows.

Jessie had tried to focus on cataloguing the faces of those seated in the white chairs arranged in rows on the lawn, trying to gauge who might be closest to Grant Williams, either through friendship or employment. But with Ian's warm leg pressed against hers, Jessie's mind kept wandering to what-ifs.

What if she had been born to a group of people such as these? Not because of their wealth, but because they obviously loved, supported, and protected one another.

What if she had met Ian under different circumstances?

What if she dared to take a risk, just this once, with him?

She couldn't change the past or the circumstances of her

life, but she could change how she lived in this moment. A risk taken could equal a memory, something to revisit in the dark of night.

"I'm good. I think getting out of here is a great idea." Being the focus of attention because of people's assumptions about her and Ian wasn't going to help her achieve her goal of finding out who was doing business with who in any way, shape or form. Rationalization or not, she wanted to get out of here. With Ian.

"Excellent." He slipped his hand into hers and led her off the dance floor.

His dad broke away from the group he'd been talking among and stepped in front of Ian. "You heading to the rodeo?"

Ian glanced back at her. She knew how much he hated lying to his family. She gave his hand a squeeze.

He looked back at his father. "No. We're just going to head back to the house. Did you need something?"

"No, not at all. I was just going to tell you that you didn't need to go to the rodeo for us. Liam didn't want to come to"—he waved a hand at the dance floor and milling groups of wedding attendees—"all this, so I sent him and Amanda to the rodeo grounds to be there for the guys if they need anything." He smiled indulgently between her and Ian. "You kids go have fun."

"Thanks, Dad." Ian clapped his father on the shoulder and walked past him.

Jessie had no idea what to say to the elder Neisson, so she simply smiled her goodbyes as she allowed Ian to tug her toward the path leading to the parking area where his truck was.

Ian appeared to think of something and paused, drawing her up short. "Do you need to go into the house for anything before we hit the road?"

She knew he was thinking of the rest room, but Jessie's brain immediately went to Grant's home office, which she'd probably never find without attracting attention.

"No, I'm fine. Let's go."

He smiled. "Okay. Let's go." He threaded his fingers through hers in a way that melted the ice around Jessie's heart.

Right then, at that moment, she would have followed him anywhere.

Fortunately, she only had to follow him to the big Wright Ranch truck. And to the ranch manager's house she was stupidly starting to think of as home.

Ian helped her into the passenger captain's seat, his warm touch lingering on her arm, her waist, and her thigh where he tucked the skirt of her dress up out of the way of the door before he closed it. All the while she felt his dark blue eyes hot on her.

Other parts of Jessie began to melt also.

She felt her phone vibrate inside her clutch on her lap. She took it out and saw a text from Peter.

All good?

She glanced at Ian, doing a poor job of ignoring her.

All good. Heading back to Wright Ranch.

Peter texted back the thumbs-up emoji. He was either

feeling more comfortable working with her, or he was losing his mind in the Pineville Motel.

She must have made a noise because Ian glanced at her. "Everything okay?"

"Yep."

He shifted in his seat. "So . . . You and Peter . . ." He left the leading question hanging.

He asks now? After kissing her more than once?

"Are just coworkers. He has a very nice significant other who I like a lot."

The brim of Ian's hat tipped as he nodded. "Okay. Cool." Then he grinned. "Just thought I'd check."

"After you kissed me." She laughed.

"Because I intend on kissing you again. You good with that?"

Heat flashed through her, and it was her turn to shift in her seat. "Considering I kissed you first, I think the answer is pretty obvious."

"A gentleman always makes sure."

A *cowboy* always makes sure. At least Ian Neisson's type of cowboy.

He caught her gaze with his hot one and her hand with his. She promptly went up in flames.

Knowing what was coming made the ride from the Bar W to the Wright Ranch pretty much a blur. While they talked of bongos and outdoor weddings, Jessie's attention was firmly on Ian. His size, his strength, his selflessness.

She had to acknowledge she'd never wanted a man more in her life.

The next thing she knew he was shutting off the truck in the driveway of the Wright Ranch's ranch manager's house, hopping out, and hurrying around the hood to open her door for her.

A couple of months ago, the move would have annoyed her.

Today it made her smile.

She took his hand and allowed him to help her out of the truck, which he did by sliding her down his body. Her gaze jumped to his, and she found him watching her. The man was beautiful. Flat-out beautiful.

He slipped a hand up the side of her neck and into her hair, holding her in place as he dropped his mouth to hers and captured her in a toe-curling kiss.

Because she'd been thinking about kissing Ian again the entire ride home—there she went, thinking of this place as home again—she wrapped both arms around his neck, knocking his cowboy hat askew with her clutch. She would have collapsed back into the cab of the truck if he hadn't braced his feet wide and anchored her to him with one hand splayed in her hair and the other low on her back.

He deepened the kiss, his tongue touching hers in a way that ignited a storm of passion in Jessie.

Ian pulled away. "I need to get you inside."

"Same."

He laughed and scooped her up in his arms, pausing long enough to kick the truck door shut with his boot. He carried her to the front door as if she weighed nothing. "Can you get the latch?"

"It's not locked?"

He snorted. "Did you not notice that gate we came through?"

She reached for the door and opened it, squeaking when he hoisted her higher in his arms so he could use his elbow to push the door all the way open. "But what about the acres—"

"Miles," he corrected, shoving the door closed again with his backside once they were through.

"Sheesh, okay, miles of fence line that anyone could climb?"

He headed down the hall, his boot heels loud on the slate. "And find themselves in the middle of a field of rank bucking bulls. My grandfather likes to keep them close to the house so he doesn't have to go far to check on them."

"Beware of bull?"

"You got it."

She laughed, but sobered when she realized Ian had carried her into his bedroom. His bed was huge, four-poster, and made of dark wood, with a dark brown suede-looking comforter. The wall opposite the door was almost entirely windows, with a French door opening out onto the deck right next to the hot tub. She hadn't noticed the doors when she'd been out in the tub with him after their day of riding. Her attention had been entirely on the breathtaking view offered by both the man and the mountains.

Ian walked to the tall bed and set her down gently. The incredibly soft comforter and mound of pillows enveloped her. When he tried to straighten away she kept her grip on his neck. She wanted him on the bed with her. On her.

"I need to take my boots off, Jess."

She gave him a wicked grin. "Do you?"

He grinned back and kissed her, but pulled away before she could distract him. "Yes. I do." He dropped a kiss on the tip of her nose, a simple act that overwhelmed her completely with all the warm and squishy feels.

It dawned on her that she still had her clutch in one hand, so she tossed it onto the closest nightstand. She raised her arms above her head, luxuriating in the feel of the comforter beneath her and the sight of the beautiful man above her as he pulled his hat from his head and flipped it onto the nightstand atop her clutch while he toed his boots off. Almost in the same motion, he shed his blazer, dropping it on the floor, quickly followed by his shirt, which he only took the time to unbutton partway before pulling it over his head.

Jessie sucked in a breath at the sight of his sculpted chest and chiseled abs. Both of which she had seen before, but now she was about to touch them. Her fingers itched with need, along with other places on her body that hadn't felt that particular itch in a long while.

Just the thought had her reaching up toward him.

He stopped in the act of unfastening the silly belt she'd bought him and collapsed down onto the bed next to her. He settled one leg between hers, making her suck in a breath, then ran his hands up her arms, which had her hissing out the very same breath.

Ian threaded his fingers between hers, rocked his hips forward, and kissed her long and deep.

Swamped by heat and sensation, Jessie arched against Ian, and he shifted more of his weight onto her. She was consumed by the need to rub against every hard inch of him. But there was something a little too hard that needed to come off.

She pulled back from his kiss to say, "Okay, today I don't have to ask if that's your belt buckle, or if you're happy to see me."

His blond brows dipped for a moment, then realization dawn clearly on his face. "But the answer would be yes. On both counts." He released her hands and rolled away from her. "I'm sorry. I somehow got distracted while taking it off." He stood and unfastened the belt and unfastened his slacks.

He hesitated, his gaze meeting hers.

Jessie swallowed and nodded. "I'll be overdressed, but ditch 'em, cowboy."

"You won't be overdressed for long," he said and started to push his slacks down, but then he stopped, his gaze going to the windows. "I'm just going to close these . . ." he said as he went to the windows and pulled the heavy, dark brown drapes closed. "Just in case someone comes looking for me." He also went to the bedroom door and shut it, turning the lock.

Considering his front—and now that she thought about it—back door were usually left unlocked, she appreciated the courtesy.

Ian came back to the side of the bed and shucked his slacks and boxers in one motion.

She choked at the glorious sight of him. "So that wasn't

just your belt buckle."

"I told you as much," he said as he climbed back onto the bed and stretched his long, muscular body out next to her. "This is a very pretty dress, but it needs to go."

"Yes, please." She sat up and twisted so he could reach the zipper she'd only just been able to get closed when she'd dressed this morning.

Ian's fingers were hot as he guided the zipper down, revealing her skin in increments that he kissed as her dress parted.

Jessie had never been so hot but shivery in her entire life.

Once he'd completely unzipped her dress, he slowly pushed it from her shoulders. Her bra came off with it, and only then did she realize he'd deftly unfastened it.

"Lie back," he instructed.

She complied, and he guided the dress down over her hips, snagging her panties and removing them along with it. Her low-heeled sandals were the last to go, being tossed off the end of the bed with the rest of her clothes.

As he climbed back up her, his heat enveloping her, she was gripped by a sudden nervousness that had her saying, "That was a very efficient way to get naked."

"That's me, Mr. Efficient." He paused, his hand poised just below her breast. "Was that okay? If not, I can redress you and try again with more class."

Her nervousness fled and she laughed. She reached for his tousled hair, burying her fingers deep in the surprisingly silky mass. "No, no. Efficiency, in this case in particular, is a very good thing," she murmured and drew his mouth back to hers, kissing him deeply.

Each kiss was more tinder on the fire he'd ignited in her. She wanted this man. She wanted him now.

Hooking her foot around his calf, she urged him on top of her, reveling in his weight, his heat.

Bearing most of his weight on his elbows, Ian broke off their kiss and pulled back enough to look down at her. He didn't say anything, but the question, the need for permission, was clear in his stunning blue eyes.

Jessie slid her hands down to cup his strong jaw, his emerging beard bristly against her palms. "Please make love to me, Ian."

He dropped one, two, three quick kisses on her mouth, then smiled the sexiest, sweetest, most heart-rending smile she'd ever seen. "Yes, ma'am."

Jessie decided, right then and there, that being ma'amed was her new most favorite thing.

CHAPTER FOURTEEN

J ESSIE WOKE THE next morning with the heat of Ian's big
body pressed into her back and a storm of emotions raging
inside of her. If she had had any idea the impact spending a
night in Ian's arms would have had on her, she would have
hightailed it back to the motel after the wedding. She never
would have risked it.

Now it was too late. Way too late.

The moist heat of Ian's lips placing featherlight kisses on
the back of her neck let her know he was awake too. That
and another thing.

She couldn't help but squirm her hips slightly against
him. She felt him smile against her skin.

Contentment expanded in her chest until she could
hardly breathe.

The notification ping of a text coming through on a cell
phone sounded.

Ian groaned into her hair.

"Is that you?" she asked.

"Yes. It's been going off for a while. I'm impressed you
slept through it."

She scoffed. "I don't know about you, but I'm tired. I

had some gorgeous cowboy keeping me up all night."

He chuckled and nuzzled his way toward her ear. "That's because you kept *me* up." He shifted his hips toward her, making it clear exactly what he meant by *up*.

His phone pinged again.

"Aren't you going to get that? It might be something critical."

"I don't care. I'm not leaving this bed. Besides, whoever it was would have called if it was something critical. And odds are it's more than one person texting me, wondering where I am."

"The price of being a control freak?" she joked, guiding his hand on one of the paths it had taken during the night. Her skin responded instantly, pebbling with a shiver of pleasure.

"I am not a control freak. I'm a control aficionado." He nibbled on her earlobe.

She laughed and raised her shoulder in defense against the tickling sensation created by his teeth. "Control aficionado. I like that. Can I steal it?"

His tongue took over for his teeth. "You can steal anything you want from me."

Including your heart?

The unbidden, not to mention unexpected, thought popped into Jessie's brain. And once there, she couldn't shake it. But she didn't want Ian's heart, any more than she wanted him to steal hers. Right?

Another text came in.

"You really should check your phone. It'll drive me crazy

if you don't."

He rolled away from her to snag his phone off the nightstand he'd put it on at some point in the night. "I'll just put it on silent."

"It's not the noise that bugs me, it's the wondering what's happening."

"You're a need-to-know aficionado." He picked up the cell phone and flicked his thumb across the screen.

She laughed again. "That I am. And because of it, I need to check my own phone to see if Peter tracked down the source of a pending sale of cows to Grant Williams's bull breeding operation." She pulled the sheet up to help her brain shift into work mode and away from the quivering pile of need Ian had reduced her to, then reached for her clutch on the nightstand next to her.

"Don't you mean the cows Grant is going to sell to Jacob Hadley to replace the ones stolen from the Hadleys' breeding program?"

"Nope. These are cows coming in, not going out. His brand requested new tag registrations, but without the complete sale information."

Ian was silent for a long moment. "You know, I think I'd better deal with this after all." Phone in hand, Ian swung his legs off the other side of the bed.

She stopped in the act of fishing her phone out of her clutch long enough to watch Ian's backside as he walked into the bathroom. She sighed in contentment. There was nothing in the world like a cowboy butt.

He closed the bathroom door and Jessie returned her attention to her phone, which she always kept on silent. There was only one text and it was from Peter.

You good?

She smiled. She was definitely good. She texted back, *I'm good.*

Peter texted, *Need to get out of motel. Going to work at the sheriff's.*

Roger that, she acknowledged him.

The bathroom door opened and Ian emerged wearing jeans and a blue checked shirt he was buttoning up. Both looked like they'd been in a hamper.

Jessie sat up, clutching the sheet over her breasts. "Wha—?"

"I have to go." Ian barely glanced at her as he went to his walk-in closet and emerged with a pair of beat-up brown cowboy boots. "I'll talk to you later." And then he was gone.

Jessie heard him stomp his way into his boots before leaving through the sliding glass door. She was tempted to jump from the bed and run to the drawn curtains to watch to see if he was heading up the path to the stable, or the main house, or somewhere else on the massive ranch, but she forced herself to remain where she was.

And berated herself for falling under the spell of a cowboy.

IT WAS NEARLY dinnertime when Jessie finally looked up from the spreadsheet she had been staring blindly at. Seated across the table from her in the sheriff's office interrogation room, Peter was rubbing his eyes.

"Why don't you take a break?" she said. "You've been at this way longer than I have, and I'm already going cross-eyed."

Peter had already been at the sheriff's station when she'd called him and asked him to come pick her up. Fortunately, the keypad on the huge front gate to the ranch allowed for Peter to contact the ranch manager's house directly so she could buzz him through.

"Good idea." Peter pushed back from the table and stood. "Do you want anything from the vending machine? Or more coffee?"

"Thanks, but no." She hadn't had much of an appetite all day, and regret was creating enough acid in her stomach that the last thing she needed was more coffee. She'd really crossed the line with Ian the night before, and she'd hoped burying herself in work would help.

It hadn't.

She'd checked her phone constantly throughout the day, but Ian never called or texted. She couldn't decide which made her angrier, that he hadn't contacted her or that it mattered to her. And it wasn't as if she had tried to call or text him. She hadn't. She was working. And she needed to stay focused.

Peter reappeared in the doorway of the small room. "Hey, look who I found." He stepped into the room.

Ian appeared behind Peter. His gaze met hers briefly, his blue eyes clouded. By worry? Or maybe concern. Because he hadn't contacted her?

She told herself she didn't care if he was worried or concerned about her and sat back in the metal chair, crossing her arms over her chest. He looked back down the hall and gestured to someone. A much shorter, older man stepped into the interrogation room. The sheriff also appeared in the doorway and leaned his shoulder against the jamb.

Something was up. She sat up in her chair, going into alert mode.

Ian followed, saying, "Special Agent Martin, Special Agent Beck, this is Stan Davies. Stan has a cattle ranch about fifty miles east of here."

Peter shook the man's hand. Jessie also reached up and shook his hand. Her gaze darted to the big cowboy beside him. What was Ian doing?

Ian said, "Earlier . . . when you mentioned the new group of cows coming into Grant's breeding program, it reminded me of something I'd heard about and wanted to check out. Tell the agents what you told me, Stan," Ian encouraged the rancher.

Jessie blinked. So Ian hadn't bolted out on her earlier because of any text he'd received. He'd left to try to help her. A warmth that started suspiciously in the area of her heart spread through her like a drop of oil in a puddle of water.

Stan removed his work-worn baseball cap and worried it between his hands. "Almost a month ago, a man came out to my ranch wanting to buy my whole herd of proven calving cows. But I'm trying to build my herd, and that's pretty tough to do without proven cows, so I told him no and sent him on his way."

Jessie uncrossed her arms and leaned forward.

"It wasn't a week later that I discovered the majority of the herd had gone missing from the Bureau of Land Management land where I have a grazing lease."

Jessie pulled a pad of paper close and made a note of the dates. "Did you report the theft, Mr. Davies?"

He dropped his gaze and shook his head. "No. That section of range is really in the middle of nowhere. I just figured they'd wandered off and it was simply a matter of me finding them. But I've ridden every inch of that land, and those cows are nowhere to be found."

Ian pulled his phone from his pocket and touched the screen. He held the image that appeared up to Mr. Davies. "Is this the man who came to your ranch wanting to buy the cows?"

Mr. Davies pulled a pair of reading glassed from his shirt pocket and donned them to peer at Ian's phone. He nodded immediately. "Yep." He pointed a thick finger at the phone and nodded again. "That's him."

Ian turned the phone so the screen faced her. Her brows shot up and her gaze sought Ian's.

He said, "I asked Grant for the picture."

Peter said, "Let me see."

Ian handed him the phone, and Peter frowned down at the photo on the screen. "A wedding picture?" He looked at her. "Is this from yesterday?"

She nodded, a bubble of excitement forming in her chest.

"Is this who Grant Williams's daughter married?" Peter asked, his gaze bouncing between her and Ian.

"Lance Powel," Jessie supplied, gesturing for Peter to give her the phone. "Not only is he now Grant Williams's son-in-law, but he is also Grant's ranch manager."

Peter's eyes rounded. "We got him."

By him, Jessie knew Peter was referring to Grant Williams. She grinned. All the work they'd put in over the last almost six months, all the time they'd spent slogging through currency transaction reports at the sheriff's office and in the Pineville Motel was finally paying off.

Ian shook his head. "Grant isn't involved, Jess."

The sheriff straightened away from the door jamb. "I'm inclined to agree with Ian. Before he caught Lillian's eye, Lance was nothing more than a ranch hand—"

"And not a very good one," Ian interjected.

The sheriff nodded and continued, "A bad ranch hand who everyone agrees seduced Lillian."

Jessie set Ian's phone carefully on the table in front of her. Seeing it in real life, Jessie had assumed the self-satisfied smirk on Lance's face had been from landing the rich rancher's daughter. Now she read so much more into the look.

Ian moved closer to Jessie. "Because of all the ranches he's bounced around working for, he's bound to have extensive knowledge of the ION territory."

"He's also a known associate of Karl Fletcher," the sheriff said.

The man who'd stolen from Ian's grandfather and set

angry bulls on Ian's mother, sister, and cousin.

Jessie's heart pinched.

Ian grunted. "That explains how Fletch was able to get a job working at Grant's."

"And how he got such easy access to Kraken and Night-shade, the bulls that almost killed Caitlin at the beginning of the summer," the sheriff said then scrubbed a hand over his face.

Ian made a noise that sounded suspiciously like a growl. Jessie had an intense urge to reach out and snag his hand, to hold it and offer comfort. Luckily, he moved his hands from her reach by crossing his arms over his chest. The chest she'd been snuggled against just this morning.

Her cheeks grew warm and she dropped her gaze to the photo on the phone, using her fingers to enlarge the image of Lance's face. Jessie was seized with the need to get the guy and make him pay.

Ian said, "With all the new connections and deep pockets provided by his new father-in-law's operation, Lance Powel has ample means and opportunity for rustling, if he were inclined."

Mr. Davies interjected, "Which he clearly was."

"Would you be willing to make a statement regarding Lance Powel's visit to your ranch and subsequent loss of your cattle?" Peter asked the older rancher.

Mr. Davies returned his cap to his head and gave the bill a tug. "If it'll help lock that SOB. up, then you bet."

"I can take his statement," the sheriff said. "Let's go to my office, Mr. Davies."

Before he left, Jessie stood and offered him her hand. "Thank you for your help, Mr. Davies. It's truly invaluable."

He shook her hand. "My pleasure, ma'am."

As she watched Mr. Davies leave with the sheriff, Jessie thought that with the arrest of Lance Powel they would be putting a huge dent in the area's livestock theft problem.

And would earn her the right to request a transfer to a major city.

The fact should make her ecstatic.

It didn't.

The looming, magnetic presence of the big man next to her gave her a sinking feeling that she knew exactly why.

IAN HAD THOUGHT that handing Jessie the likely key player in the Idaho, Oregon, and Nevada territory rustling ring on a silver platter would have made her happy. But it hadn't. She didn't look happy. She looked annoyed.

Maybe he should have simply steered her in the direction of Stan Davies, whose loss of livestock had been whispered about around town. But because Stan himself had staunchly denied the rumor, Ian hadn't wanted to say anything until he could be sure by driving down to Stan's spread and showing him Lance's picture—conveniently available thanks to the wedding photos. As soon as Stan realized the thief could actually be caught with his help, he'd been more than willing to cooperate.

Ian had known Lance was a shady character, but the timing of his acquisition of a herd of sought-after cows on the heels of Stan's loss had raised Ian's suspicions.

Satisfied he'd done right by his family and community, if not necessarily by Jessie, Ian offered her his hand with the intention of wishing her well. He knew how badly she wanted to get out of Podunk Pineville by being reassigned to the biggest, least rural city she could find.

She stared down at his hand as if he were offering her a handful of steaming cow shit.

Peter cleared his throat. "Um, I'm just going to go and . . . and make sure the sheriff is getting all the pertinent facts."

Jessie ignored her fellow agent, her gaze fixed on Ian's outstretched hand.

Clearly uncomfortable, Peter said, "Right. I'll just . . ." He didn't finish, instead simply hurried from the room.

While Ian was watching Peter leave the interrogation room, Jessie gripped his hand in hers and gave it a firm shake.

He didn't let go.

The second her palm contacted his, the second they'd touched skin to skin, again, Ian knew he couldn't say goodbye to this woman. But after what she'd told him of her childhood on her stepfather's ranch and of how hard she'd worked to escape that world, he couldn't ask her to stay with him on his family's ranch.

And he couldn't leave to go with her. He had a vow to keep.

He was, officially, screwed.

She finally raised those spring grass-colored eyes of hers to meet his and as he tumbled into them as if thrown from his horse, he knew, without a doubt, exactly why he was so utterly screwed.

He had fallen in love with Special Agent Jessica Martin.

And he didn't know what to do about it.

Not used to not knowing what to do, Ian pulled his hand from hers, turned on his heel, and walked away.

THE FEEL OF Ian's palm against hers, not to mention the look of utter longing on his face, nearly knocked Jessie back into her seat. A flash of realization hit her like a bullet to her vest.

She wanted him to ask her to stay. She wanted him to ask her to remain in Pineville with him.

Because living on a ranch—any ranch, not just the Wright Ranch—with a cowboy like him would be as different from her youth as a lush forest was to the moon. She'd happily live in a tent on the back forty with Ian.

But Ian hadn't asked her to stay.

He'd simply shook her hand and walked away.

The pain of loss took her breath away. Now what was she going to do?

CHAPTER FIFTEEN

WITH THE SWORN affidavit provided by Stan Davies, not to mention a small herd of freshly tagged cows found in a remote corner of the Bar W that matched Mr. Davies's missing herd, Jessie and Peter were able to get a search warrant for Lance Powel's personal property. They found the flash drive Karl Fletcher had told them about that contained an accounting of the livestock thefts and subsequent sales. More than enough for them to arrest Lance Powel and his cohorts, whom he quickly gave up.

Poor Lillian. The third time had not been the charm.

But Jessie found little satisfaction in the successful conclusion of the investigation.

Late at night, as she lay in her motel room bed staring up at the ceiling, she had no choice but to admit to herself, over and over, that she was in love with Ian Neisson. A cowboy's cowboy. What a world.

Too bad she feared in the marrow of her bones that she'd lost her chance with him.

Ian was a man of pride and honor. A cowboy who kept whatever vow he might make, and he'd vowed to put his family first. A vow he'd diligently kept for a decade.

But Jessie hadn't achieved as much as she had thus far in her life by giving up on what she wanted.

And she wanted Ian.

More than she'd wanted anything else in her life.

Two weeks to the day from the last time she'd seen Ian, Jessie placed a call to her superior, Special Agent in Charge Michael Truman.

Though SAC Truman at first thought she was joking when she asked if there was any way she could remain in Pineville, setting up a sort of satellite office for the bureau to monitor the ION territory, once she'd convinced him of her seriousness, he'd expressed interest. But he wouldn't commit until budget constraints could be addressed.

Jessie stared at her cell after ending the call. She just wasn't sure the possibility that she might being able to stay in Pineville would be enough to win over Ian.

His family was everything to him.

Maybe that's where she should start.

Once again driving the borrowed unmarked sheriff's truck, Jessie drove out to the Wright Ranch. But this time she buzzed the main house to be let through the gate. Parking in the circular drive, she made her way up the walk to the big house's massive front door, tugging on the jacket of her sensible gray work suit. She wasn't coming here as anything other than herself, so she'd dressed appropriately this time.

She pulled in a determined breath and knocked on the big solid door. It was opened almost immediately by Alec, barefoot in jeans and a white T-shirt, with a huge ice pack balanced on his shoulder, the clearly injured arm held tight across his stomach. He must have been the one who'd buzzed her through the main gate.

"Jessie!" Alec smiled wide and stepped forward to offer her a one-handed hug.

Her throat tightened as she returned the lanky young man's hug. Would he hate her for lying to him? The possibility made her stomach churn.

"Hey, Alec." She stepped back and gestured to the ice pack. "You okay?"

"I'm fine." He waved her concern off and ushered her into the house. "Just landed wrong."

"Is there a right way to land after being bucked off a bull?"

He grinned as he shut the door. "Yeah. It's called not getting bucked off in the first place."

"Or not getting on the bull in the first place?"

"Not an option." He winked. "You looking for Ian? I haven't seen him this morning. But I haven't been out of the main house yet." He readjusted the ice pack.

She gripped her hands together in front of her. "Actually, no. I was hoping to be able to see your grandfather."

Alec's dark blond brows went up. "Granddad? Sure, he's here. Follow me."

Tugging on her jacket again, Jessie followed Alec as he padded to the hallway that bisected the house, turning toward the right wing.

He stopped at an open doorway on the left. "Hey, Granddad. Ian's Jessie is here to see you. Are you free?"

Ian's Jessie.

Her heart stuttered at the moniker.

A deep voice within the room said, "Absolutely. Send her in."

Alec stepped to the side and hitched his head toward the room. "He's all yours."

"Thanks, Alec," she said softly as she passed him to step into what turned out to be Thomas Wright's home office. The man himself was seated behind a huge desk that faced the door, a wall of windows offering a view of green pastures and mountains at his back and built-in bookshelves and cabinetry on either side.

"No problem." Alec tipped an imaginary hat to her then disappeared back down the hall.

"Miss Martin," Thomas exclaimed with a smile. He pushed his overstuffed leather chair back from the desk and rose, then rounded the desk. Wearing a tan suede western-style blazer, dark brown slacks, and a bolo tie over his white button-down shirt, Thomas Wright was the very picture of the gentleman rancher. Or cattle baron. Both fit the very impressive older man.

Jessie extended her hand, expecting a handshake, but Thomas instead pulled her in for a brief hug. The show of familiarity stunned her and added to her anxiety. She really doubted Thomas Wright appreciated being lied to. But she had to find out if she could have a future here if she was to have any hope at all with Ian.

"What can I do for you this morning?" he asked.

"I'd like to talk to you, if you have a moment."

"Of course. Please, have a seat." He gestured to one of two matching nail-head leather chairs that faced his desk.

"Thank you," she said and perched on the edge of the chair. She was too nervous to relax back into the plush seat.

Thomas went back around the desk and retook his seat, leaning forward with clear attentiveness.

"Sir—"

"Please, call me Thomas."

Her mouth went completely dry, but she nodded. "Thomas, I don't know if you remember me mentioning that I attended law school."

"I do." He smiled indulgently, but his blue eyes, much lighter than Ian's, were razor sharp.

"While it's been a while since I practiced, I am still licensed, and . . . well—"

"Just spit it out, girl." Thomas leaned back into his chair, tenting his fingers in front of himself. "How can I help you?"

Like Ian, Thomas Wright was ready, and uniquely able, to help solve the problems of the people around him. She really hated that she'd very recently thought so poorly of him. Guilt heated her cheeks.

She gripped her hands together in her lap. "I was wondering if there would be any way for me to act as your lawyer, or your family's lawyer, so that I can help Ian serve the family?"

Thomas pursed his lips together, then shook his head. "No."

The one word had the power to knock all the air from Jessie's lungs. "No?" Panic swelled up into her throat.

"No," he repeated succinctly. "Would you like to know why?"

Here it came, the consequences of her lies. "Please."

"Because I'd rather have an FBI agent in the family than a lawyer."

Jessie's jaw went slack as she tried to process what Thomas had just said. "You know?"

"I *knew*," he corrected and pushed himself up from his chair.

"Grandfather always knows," a deep voice said behind her. Ian.

Jessie's heart shuddered. How would she ever get him back now?

IAN DRANK IN the sight of Jessie Martin, seated before his grandfather's desk in the spot usually reserved for come to Jesus moments. The morning sun streaming in through the wall of windows in his grandfather's office glinted off her midnight-black hair, begging for his hand.

He had made it an entire week before he'd decided he couldn't live without her, then it had taken him another week to figure out how best to win her.

Turned out the truth was the key.

A no-brainer in his world, actually.

And the first stop on the truth train had been in this very room, with his dad and grandfather present.

Despite his fears and concerns, both men had been receptive and supportive. In no small part because his grandfather had already known Jessie's true identity and purpose for being here. And wanting the thieves caught as badly as Ian had, his grandfather had gone along with the ruse.

If only Ian had known.

But would he have arrived at the place he found himself now, desperately in love with this woman and fully ready to face the risk that loving someone so much entailed?

He didn't know and he didn't care. All that mattered was winning her once and for all.

JESSIE TWISTED IN her seat to find Ian standing in the doorway, watching her.

While his grandfather was the epitome of the wealthy rancher with impeccable clothing style and confidence, Ian was the picture of the successful working cowboy. His light brown cowboy boots were scuffed and worn, his jeans, though clean, bore the sort of whiskering that came only from hours in the saddle. And while his oiled canvas barn jacket was of obvious quality, its practicality was undeniable. He'd pulled his cowboy hat from his head and was tapping it against his muscular thigh.

Thomas rounded the desk, saying, "Now if you'll excuse me, I have paperwork that needs to be seen to in the bull barn." He stopped next to Jessie long enough to place a hand on her shoulder and give a gentle squeeze. "Welcome to the family, Special Agent Martin."

Jessie could only gape at his retreating back.

Thomas gave his eldest grandson a similar touch before disappearing out the door and down the hall.

Her gaze collided with Ian's and found him watching her even more intently.

Stunned confusion made her heart rate do a two-step in her chest. She asked, "Welcome to the family?"

Ian strode forward, taking the chair that matched the one she occupied. "He has already scolded me about not having locked you down already."

She blinked. She wasn't sure if she should be insulted or delighted. "Locked me down? Scolded you?" She was really having a hard time getting her brain to work. "Did you tell him who I really was and why I was here?"

"I did." There wasn't a scrap of repentance on his handsome face. "I also told him exactly how I feel about you."

Jessie's heart began to race wildly as she searched his blue eyes. Dare she hope he felt the same way about her as she did about him?

She leaned toward him. "How you feel . . . ?" She was either losing her mind or becoming a parrot. But she couldn't seem to grasp what she was hearing.

Ian reached out and peeled her hands apart then drew one toward him so he could hold it in both of his. His thumb rhythmically stroked the sensitive spot at the base of her thumb. "I've fallen in love with you, Jess. I want to be with you. I'll go wherever your next assignment ends up being. I don't care where I live, as long as I'm with you."

"But your family—"

"Will always be my family. I don't have to be here to be a part of their lives. And I have the right to live my own life. Grandfather reminded me that the best way to honor my mother is by being as happy as I can be." He looked down at her hand in his, ridiculously pale against his suntanned skin. "You, Jessica Martin, make me happy." He raised his gaze to hers again and her breath caught at what she saw. "Holy shit, you make me happy. I love you, Jess," he repeated thickly. "I want to be with you. Forever."

Jessie's vision swam. "I love you, too, Ian. And I want to be with you. I've never wanted anything more in my life."

Ian squeezed his eyes shut and brought her hand to his lips and kissed her knuckles with more love and tenderness than she'd ever experienced in her entire life.

"But—"

His gaze leapt to hers. "But?"

"Is there any chance we can stay here? At the Wright Ranch? Your family really doesn't suck." She tried for levity, but the quaver in her voice spoiled it.

"What about your career?"

Her love for him grew more than she thought possible. "I called my SAC—special agent in charge—basically my boss, this morning and asked him if I could stay here, in Pineville. Establish a satellite office of sorts to keep an eye on the ION territory. He needs to crunch the numbers first, of course, but he was very receptive to the idea."

She reached to cover his hands with her free one. "Assuming you're okay with me still being FBI. If not, I can go back to practicing law—"

Ian gathered both her hands in his and squeezed them gently. "I want you to do what makes you happy. From what I've seen, that's being a special agent." He grinned at her, and she felt the impact of his smile on her soul. "I'm totally good with having a complete badass in my bed."

She had to blink rapidly to keep the tears in her eyes from streaming down her cheeks.

"Honestly, Jess. I don't care what you do. As long as you agree to be mine forever. Because I will love you forever."

She half sobbed, half hiccupped. "Cross your heart?"

He leaned forward and kissed her, sweetly, tenderly. He pulled back and met her gaze and suddenly she was looking right at her deepest, most secret desire. "Cross my heart. And that's one vow I can easily keep."

THE END

Want more? Check out Amanda and Liam's story in *Wrangling the Cowboy's Heart*!

Join Tule Publishing's newsletter for more great reads and weekly deals!

If you enjoyed *The Cowboy's Vow*,
you'll love the other books in....

THE RODEO ROMEOS SERIES

Book 1: *The Bull Rider's Second Chance*

Book 2: *Wrangling the Cowboy's Heart*

Book 3: *The Cowboy's Vow*

Available now at your favorite online retailer!

ABOUT THE AUTHOR

Having never met an unhappy ending she couldn't mentally "fix," Leah Vale believes writing romance novels is the perfect job for her. A Pacific Northwest native with a B.A. in Communications from the University of Washington, she lives in Central Oregon, with a huge golden retriever who thinks he's a lap dog. While having the chance to share her "happy endings from scratch" is a dream come true, dinner generally has to come premade from the store.

Thank you for reading

THE COWBOY'S VOW

If you enjoyed this book, you can find more from all our great authors at TulePublishing.com, or from your favorite online retailer.

TULE
PUBLISHING

Made in the USA
Columbia, SC
04 May 2021